THE LONELINESS
OF THE
DEEP SPACE
CARGOIST

JS CARTER GILSON
THE LONELINESS OF THE DEEP SPACE CARGOIST

Cavia 🐹 Porcellus

Nashua, NH

Cavia Porcellus
Nashua, NH

ISBN   978-1-95504-500-1

LCCN 2020907778

Design by Cavia Porcellus.
Cover features illustrations furnished by Pond 5,
http://www.pond5.com/

For Mary Ellen,
my heart.

Going to a place that's far
So far away and if that's not enough
Going where nobody says hello
Don't talk to anybody they don't know

—*R.E.M.,* (Don't Go Back to) Rockville

1

Inez Stanton was on the john when the siren started going off. She slapped the comms panel next to her and a cheerful voice rang out, "Saluti, comandante." Great, something fucked up the language control.

"What's happening?" she said, a little startled at the loudness of her own voice. How long since she had spoken out loud?

"Мы пострадали от мусора." It took a few seconds for Inez to remember her Russian. Debris. Shit.

"Where were we hit?"

"Rahtikotelossa." Was that, fuck, Finnish? Still, given that the ship wasn't actually destroyed, it was probably the cargo hold.

Inez finished cleaning up and pulled up her jumpsuit. She grabbed the fire extinguisher from the dull metallic corridor wall and approached the door to the hold.

"I hate to ask this, gods know how you'll respond. Is there air pressure in the cargo hold?"

"Les barrières tiennent."

Right. So, she could breathe. She grabbed a respirator anyway and opened the inner door and peered through the outer door's porthole. Immediately, she could see there was no upper bulkhead over about a third of the hold, furthest from her. It looked like it must have been a glancing blow more than anything, though, because none of the cargo was even disturbed.

"How long will the barriers hold?"

"Tilu dinten, di speed urang ayeuna."

That was no help. She closed the door to the cargo hold and put the respirator and fire extinguisher back. She crossed the hundred feet to the cab and opened the door there.

"Thank you, whoever there is to thank," she whispered, seeing that her panels were still in English. So, just a bit over three days, as long as nothing else had gotten jarred loose with the hit. She pulled up the star maps to see if there was anywhere to go that was less than three days away. Fang's Waystation was going to be the closest, about two and a half days away. It would be tight, but she'd make it if nothing else went wrong.

"Why did you think that?" she whispered at herself.

She set a new course for the waystation, and killed the siren. It was giving her a headache.

She marched back out through the storage room to the closet that held a lot of the most important parts of the ship. These included the air recycler, the power cells that controlled everything but the drive core, and the ship's computer. The computer was literally the smallest part of what was in the closet.

Inez pulled out the data core of the computer and turned it over in her hands. It was a small crystal cube with a hole on one side. No obvious physical damage (though she was by no means an expert). She grabbed a test lead from next to the computer and plugged it in. The core lit up and she could see the test sequence running properly. She plugged it back into the main computer, and, after a few minutes, it began the slow blink that showed it was ready.

"What's your status?" she asked the computer.

"Working at 89% of nominal."

It was kind of amazing that rebooting was all that it took. She wiped her brow. She was sweating, despite the temperature in the rig being a constant 20 degrees. "Good. Can you monitor our progress to the waystation?"

"Pêgirtî, serwer."

Fuck. She stowed the core back into the computer case and closed the closet door. Hard.

● ■ ■ ■ ━━━━ ■ ■ ━ ıɩ((◉))ıı ━ ■ ■ ━━━━ ■ ■ ■ ●

Inez had been driving this rig for about seven years now. It wasn't fancy, and it sure as hell wasn't paid off yet, but it was as much of a home as she'd had in her life, the longest she'd slept in one bed since she was a child.

It was an older model ship, older than she was, and it was held together in parts with alutape and prayer. The dancing figure of Saint Camilia on the main console was hiding a bullet hole. Both the bullet hole and Camilia, patron saint of smugglers, pre-dated her ownership of the rig. Inez just needed a way to get away.

She turned off the music she was listening to. There was a hum in the ship that seemed just a bit louder than normal, but she really didn't know if it was actually louder, or if she was just paranoid. Not that it couldn't be both. It could always be both.

Getting the hell away from people was the whole reason she started as a cargoist. It was quiet work where she didn't need to interact with anyone much unless she wanted to. She didn't really like people, to be honest. There were some deep-seated trust issues where that was concerned, and she wasn't shy about warning anyone who showed any interest in her about it.

Out here, there was just the ever-expanding future and the ever-expanding universe. Inez was comforted by the fact that the universe would go out with a quiet sigh rather than the explosive end that she had wished for when she was younger.

Inez's upbringing was probably common under the Free Earth. She preferred not to think about when she was younger, or about what happened to her mother. She was just under thirty standard revs old, more than old enough to be angry at herself for ruminating. She had lots of time to think between destinations, and she spent as much time as she could not thinking.

With a few taps on the console she started a full ship-wide diagnostic, hoping for confirmation whether or not the ship was actually louder, and reading over her messages. A half dozen new directives from the Company, a mail forwarded to her from a third cousin she'd never met about some politics thing that she didn't know about (and that sounded just a bit like bullshit), compulsory Free Earth propaganda, nothing that captured her interest.

She thought that Free Earth might get a report back that she didn't spend the requisite amount of time looking at their latest. Then again, with her systems scrambled, who knew?

Inez closed her mail and pulled up a book. It was an old trashy book about a future that was now a few centuries in the past. She'd read it a few dozen times, the first time when Sara had snuck it to her from the library. Poor Sara. Reading was one of the ways she kept her brain quiet. No, nothing truly kept her brain quiet, but sometimes she could drown it out.

Books, music, vids (but never the news), anything that could stop her brain from wandering into those dark places. She even used some language immersion cubes that she'd found when she first went through the old smuggling nooks.

It was going to be a while before the full diagnostic report came in, so she made herself comfortable and held the book up to her face.

The board pinged a few minutes later, and Inez nearly dropped the book pad.

"What is it?"

"Tha luchd-dìon a 'putadh barrachd sprùilleach gu aon taobh."

Oh, for fucks'. She'd forgotten about the translator. She pulled up the message on the console. More debris, and according to the limited scans that the rig could do, they seemed to be from the same ship as the debris that hit the cargo hold.

She brought the ship to a stop, more or less (things in space were never really stopped), and felt the lurch as the inertial suppression systems compensated for dropping out of faster than light speed. She put the ship's diagnostic to full processing, figuring it better to get it sooner rather than later. This posture would hopefully keep the ship from being hit too hard by anything out there.

This was, well, she figured it couldn't be good. At the very least, a ship headed the way she was going had a catastrophic failure worse than what she was dealing with. Did it mean something? She had a healthy distrust of coincidence, but given space, that ship could have been destroyed centuries ago.

Still, it needed a look, and that was not something that the ship's scanners could do. She'd have to get the high-powered scanner that Annie had given her so long ago (okay, forgotten when she stormed out) and actually go out there. Poor Annie.

The exosuit locker was in the storage room. It was a large unit, and at some point she must have unplugged it, so that was going to take some time.

Light was going to be an issue. Her suit's lamps would be a little help, but she was really going to need the rig's docking lights if she was going to see anything. The rig had slots for sixteen salvage drones, but the one that had actually come with the rig when she bought it had nearly exploded the first time she powered it up. She hadn't been eager to replace them, and generally hadn't thought about them at all, but now, their high-powered lights and sensors would really come in handy.

Five hours to full charge. That was not going to work. Not at all. She was reading over the specs on the side of the locker. Full charge would give her sixteen hours in deep space with protection from radiation, heat, cold, vacuum, and space weevils. (There was a full pictogram panel about pushing space bugs away from you.) She figured that she wouldn't need more than two hours to get some good scans of the debris as long as she was within about a click of it.

The rig's scanners had found a concentrated section of debris, a large piece gravitationally pulling on the smaller pieces, if she had to guess. They were now hovering about 500 meters from the outer edge of that grouping, and she had turned up the debris deflectors on the rig so they wouldn't be destroyed by a rivet.

An hour and a half to wait for the suit to power up to where she'd need it. That was a lot of time to be waiting. She pulled up a music file and set an alert for 90 minutes.

89 minutes later, music was blasting throughout the rig, and Inez was bouncing around the way she'd seen teenagers doing in clubs in entertainment clips. She didn't have the glow paint or the intoxicants, and she had clothes on, but since no one was watching (maybe the Company, but fuck them), she did not care even a little bit.

The music stopped without even a fade out, and she was about six inches above the deck mid jump. She landed a little harder than she intended. Right. Time to do this thing.

Inez stood at the airlock. She felt like she needed to take a deep breath before venturing out, and reminded herself that she wasn't going underwater. This was far worse.

She liked working in space just fine, as long as there were nice, redundant bulkheads between her and the vacuum. The suit was only a couple of millimeters of fabric between her and burning, freezing, frying, imploding, exploding, and everything else that might happen this far between systems.

The air cycled out of the compartment, and the door opened. She stepped off the artificial gravity and felt its pull disappear. Her stomach lurched in a way that made her glad it was empty.

She focused on her hands. One held the booster control, and the other held the sensor. Both were feeding information into her helmet's display, but for the moment she was trying to ignore that.

She pulsed the booster and felt the gentle push from the points at her shoulders and hips. She turned back to look at the rig. The front section was basically a giant box. This was the detachable cargo hold. There was a faint blue glow across part of it, which is where the air shields were holding the vacuum at bay. The cargo section was Company property, and they were usually traded out at the endpoints. It made more sense in terms of efficiency to trade out cargo sections and head right back out. Usually, after recharging the batteries and a nice dinner, but not always.

The damage to the cargo hold didn't look any worse than she had expected. She piloted around to the other side of the vessel, where her part of the rig was, and with the sensor, she could tell that there were a few hairline cracks that would need to be addressed when she got to the waystation, but nothing that couldn't wait until then.

She looked up to where the main cluster of the other ship's wreckage was. The lights from the rig were highlighting some of the shinier pieces, and Inez nudged the booster forward.

When she was first out running cargo for the Company, she'd been in a rented rig that was rapidly running out of usability. A previously jury-rigged repair (from long before she'd been driving it) had come loose, so, being enterprising, Inez had put on the exosuit, grabbed a roll of alutape and jumped out of the airlock.

Immediately, she was frozen in place. The blackness of space wasn't what she had anticipated. It had weight. It was a three-dimensional presence, not an absence. It was trying to reach into her suit and strangle her. Space was malevolent and wanted her dead. No, worse. Space was entirely indifferent to her existence. To space, she was no different from the specks of dust flying with unchecked momentum around her.

She'd only been out in an exosuit a few more times, but that had been enough for her to develop a survival mechanism. Focus on the target. Do not lose sight of where you're going. Always make sure your rig would tell you how to get back to it. Most of all, though, make sure you stayed on target.

It took about ten minutes (according to the in-helmet clock) to get to a large piece of the debris. It was about half as tall as she was and was definitely an outer bulkhead. It had part of a number sequence that looked like a ship's registry. She had the scanner take it down. If nothing else, someone might want to know where their ship (and probably crew) died.

She avoided the jagged edges of it. Even though her suit was supposed to be able to withstand slashing and stabbing, it wasn't something she wanted to test out. There was a much larger piece about 200 meters up (there is no up in space, she chided herself, and then chided herself again for caring about that shit). She steered herself towards it, hoping for something that would tell her about the ship.

She got to the large chunk of metal, which looked twisted all out of shape. Her scan, though, said it was actually the right shape, an outer section of a large faster than light ship. This was from the propulsion system. The spherical singularity chamber was nowhere to be seen. It had probably jettisoned and sped away from the ship in order to keep from getting caught in the rest of the destruction. The drive cores could be extremely dangerous in the right situation.

She pulled in closer and saw that there was a deck and a half, and about 50 meters of corridor connected to the piece. There were also a half dozen bodies floating right along with it. Scan confirmed that they had died during the explosive decompression and likely hadn't even felt it.

She scanned the interior bulkhead, which was painted gray and had more numbers on it, but no other identification. This could have been just about any large cruiser. Even on a pleasure ship, the engineering section would be plain like this. Engineers never got to enjoy the pleasures of a pleasure ship anyway. They were an odd bunch (they had gained the nickname "bug eaters"), so they probably didn't have any interest in it.

She piloted around the end of the debris, and was now able to see the outside. This was no pleasure ship. The drab olive of the paint job (of course it was painted) would have given it away on its own, but the insignia, the logo, for fuck's sake, drove it home.

The logo was a planet with familiar continents, with a tree growing out the top and roots out the bottom, surrounded in block letters with "FREE EARTH". This was a Free Earth heavy cruiser, possibly even a dreadnought. This was a military ship, and based on the data she was getting from the scanner, all hands were lost. And recently, too. This wreckage was at most a month or two old. There were still enough air molecules (oxygen, nitrogen, carbon dioxide, water) caught in the weak gravitation of the debris to confirm that.

That logo. The more she looked at it, the more she felt like she was going to faint in the suit. Those fuckers. They couldn't just let her be, they had to--

No, she stopped herself. No, they didn't crash their ship to set up a trap for her. They were bastards and clever, but even they wouldn't be able to arrange something like that. Also, that many dead crewmembers to somehow fuck with her, well, no, that didn't seem likely.

Also, other than her (acknowledged) self-aggrandizement, it was more likely that Free Earth generally didn't have any idea that she existed. Live with yourself too long, you get an out-sized view of your own importance.

She set the scanner to look for the emergency beacon. It might have logs or something that could help. She really wanted to avoid meeting the indifferent omnipresence of space personally, the way these poor bastards did.

Half an hour later, beacon in tow, Inez was at the airlock. She had been out of sight range of the ship, but the lights and her suit helped her make her way back. It was really easy to get out of sight range. Disturbingly easy.

She shook that creeping feeling off, and closed the airlock doors behind her. Some fancier ships used permeable forcefields instead of airlocks, but present situation aside, she didn't really trust them to work. She'd seen them fail, and not just in low-budget vids. No, she was very glad that her rig had the old fashioned (practically prehistoric) physical airlock.

Once the doors sealed and the air started hissing in, the gravity kicked on. She landed in a crouch, but the beacon landed with a bone-shaking thud. Right, it was a piece of equipment about a half-ton in weight. She was glad she'd put it next to her and not above her.

The inner door creaked open and Inez was already halfway out of her exosuit. She stuffed it back into the cabinet and connected the power cell before going to her bunk and grabbing a new jumpsuit. Bathing was probably a waste of power, but she could at least have clean clothes.

She went to the cab and resumed the trip to the waystation. In all, she'd been stopped about three hours. She probably couldn't afford a lot more stops like that.

Using Annie's scanner, she made several passes to assess the damage. It looked like the data core was intact, amazingly, but the event that took out the ship seemed to have shorn off the power supply.

Inez carefully extracted the data core, a crystal cube about five centimeters across, from the shell of the beacon.

She didn't want to power the beacon directly, not yet anyway. She figured she'd probably power it up and push it out the airlock at some point, let the Free Earth reclaim its property. But she wanted to get as much as she could from it first. Also, be as far away from it as possible.

The data core was overkill. A core that size could hold zettabytes of data. It would have been wiped with every return to port and ships like this were never away from port for more than a year. Assuming that the things the Admiral had said around her were accurate. Fucking--well, he'd gotten his.

She found the I/O port on the cube and inserted the external storage lead into it. The cube lit up as the lasers shot through it. It started reading the data, but almost immediately walls shot up around it. This had some pretty heavy encryption that she knew her computer, in its current state, would never be able to decode. Even if it were working, it would probably take longer than her remaining lifetime.

This was one mystery that she was not likely to solve any time soon.

● ▪ ▪ ▪ ━━━━ ▪ ▪ ━ ıı((◉))ıı ━ ▪ ▪ ━━━━ ▪ ▪ ▪ ●

Inez had stowed the core in the vacuum locker under the restroom floor and made her way back to the cab. The damage report had to be done by now. There were only so many things to look at on this rig.

She was correct that the report was completed. She scanned over the sections. Drive core operating at 85%, that was about normal. Power reserves draining due to the barrier keeping air in the cargo hold. Looked like there was still enough to make it to the waystation. Air reserves--no, that couldn't be right.

No, it was right. When the cargo hold's upper bulkhead got ripped off, all of that air would have been sucked out into the vacuum. The air reserves would have been fairly well depleted by refilling that space.

Fuck, she thought. According to the report, she was already out of breathable air.

2

So, okay. She was still breathing. There was clearly still oxygen in the air, and the mix hadn't gotten so low that she was feeling loopy or tired (she stifled a yawn that had occurred unbidden), so there were things she could do.

The living area was pretty small, all in all, and there was just Inez there. There was the cab, where she did everything but shit and sleep, and she could make sacrifices if it came to that.

No, that was wrong. She had to eat, too. She didn't think she could fit food stores into the cab along with a makeshift john and anything else she needed. She started making preparations on the wall panel anyway in case she needed to do that, and realized maybe she was experiencing some oxygen deprivation.

"Dumbass," she whispered. These doors, within the rig, didn't seal or have forcefields the way the cargo hold did.

"Super dumbass," she whispered, turning away and going over to the cargo hold's panel. She checked the manifest for her cargo, something she rarely ever did out of just not wanting to get involved in other people's lives, and was actually a bit shocked. Biostock (unlabeled, probably cattle) being sent inert to a colony at the ass end of the Orion Arm.

Inert, which meant the creatures didn't need to breathe. The bins that they were packed in were magnetically affixed to the deck, so she could really kill two fish with one pike here.

She told the rig to pump the air from the cargo hold back into the reserve tanks. Once the atmosphere of the hold was negligible, she then had it drop the air barrier and the gravity.

Since the hold was a separate part of the rig, the doors between the rig and it were completely capable of holding up to vacuum.

Still, she had the computer file away the original plan as a last resort. She wasn't looking forward to pissing into a pot.

When Inez had first proposed the idea of being a cargoist to Zzrft, it had told her she was nuts. Zzrft was one of the few non-humans she'd run into at that point in her life. She had just gotten away from her old situation, and it had been a comforting presence. She was never quite sure about their relationship (the sex was pretty good, though), but when she brought up the subject, it definitely acted like a disappointed parent. Or jilted lover. One of those.

"You're fucking nuts," it said, using one of its tentacles to hold the beer bottle to its ingestion hole. "You think you don't need people, but you're wrong. You need people more than most humans I've met."

"You've met three of us, Zzrft."

"You know what I mean. You've got no people to go back to. And I've fucked you, meaning I can never go back to mine. Assholes."

"So I'm ruining your life?" She pointed her nearly empty beer bottle at it.

"I just don't want you to ruin yours. You'll be alone with your thoughts every second of the day. Even sleeping."

Inez downed her beer and grabbed another one from table. The beer was warm, but they were broke, so there were small sacrifices to be made.

"I can shut off my brain, buddy."

"Do you know how expensive alcohol is out there? Here we can at least make our own out of the crap that surrounds us."

"'Crap' being the grain they're paying us to harvest down here?"

"Exactly. A little toasted Secale X-cereale, some naturally occurring yeast, and you're in business. Makes the whole thing less mind-numbingly boring. And more mind-numbingly drunk."

Inez sighed. "It's pointless right now. Where the hell would I get the euan? No family to go to. No rich exes to fuck. You know I barely got out of--" She stopped herself. The beer bottle in her hand was empty again. "Barely got out of where I was with the hair on my," she paused, trying to remember the word, "head. Even when I'm done with my time here, I won't have enough for even a piece of crap rig."

"You've been looking up used rigs, haven't you?" It sighed, somehow, realizing how futile it was to talk her out of it. "Interminable loneliness."

"That's the sweetest thing anyone's ever said to me," Inez said, and promptly tipped her chair over backwards.

She had to admit, Zzrft (she sighed, poor Zzrft) had been right at first. At least on the ag planet, she had some company to get drunk with. It wasn't as much fun on her own. She'd watched about a million vids, but didn't really pay attention to them. She read, but nothing really stuck.

The thing she'd really done during her first year or so was play an old Russian game on the computer that didn't require her to think. All she had to do was find the spaces to drop blocks into. The only people she interacted with were from the Company and various waystation attendants. The Tenth Great and Glorious Browns Company was the full name, but "the Company" was just easier for Inez. She avoided Free Earthers as much as possible, and her routes didn't take her into very many non-human sectors.

After about two years, she was forced to take a passenger as her cargo (cheap for fuel, and paid well), and the week-long trip with her was a lot more fun than she'd had since the ag planet (and more sex, which could have been related), so now she would ask for people as cargo every few months.

Luckily, this was not one of those times. Other than the inert cattle, she was all by herself.

● ▪ ▪ ▪ ▬▬▬▬ ▪ ▪ ▬ ιι((⊙))ιι ▬ ▪ ▪ ▬▬▬▬ ▪ ▪ ▪ ●

An hour later, Inez was casually cataloging her medical supplies. This was something she had meant to do long before. She always figured there would be time to do it later. For some reason (like, maybe, just possibly, the giant, jagged hole), now seemed like the time.

Anti-inflammatories, antiseptics, bandages (cloth and spray-on foam), defibrillator (charged), morphine (nothing like a classic), cannabid pain killers (but only five, need to restock that). She closed the box, which had a stylized white caduceus on it with the words "Human Standard" stamped in block letters. It also said "Property of the Free Earth", which, if she was going to be honest with herself, still stung a bit. Her eyes rolled on their own. "I'm feeling solidarity with aspirin now?"

She felt a lurch in the deck and reached out to the wall to stabilize herself. There was no klaxon going off, but since she'd never had to shut the alarm off before, she wasn't sure if it had taken the whole alert system with it.

She didn't want to ask the rig what was wrong, so she stood up from her bunk and made her way back to the cab. Through the window, it looked like there was a flickering fire, and her heart lurched almost as hard as the rig had. But no, if the cab was on fire, then the fire suppression systems would have kicked in. If they were still working. Shit.

Several moments into considering her options, she finally worked up the nerve to look straight through the high, round portal. Just lights on the panels.

A lot of lights on the panels.

Shit shit shit.

She opened the door, still somewhat expecting extreme heat to attack her, but instead it was just the cool of the recycled air.

"Is there any chance I can get an answer about what that was?"

"Қоқысты болдырмас үшін курсты кенеттен түзету."

"That's what I figured." She sighed and checked the log which, like the rest of the controls, was still in English. She saw a course correction to maneuver around another large patch of debris. Even with the limited scanning ability of her rig, she could see that it was a different ship from the Free Earth dreadnought. It had a different elemental makeup, and different drive radiation levels. Just based on what she had been able to see of the last ship, this one seemed to be far older.

At least she hadn't hit it this time. The language circuits may be fried, but it was learning to avoid these things on its own.

She wasn't going to stop and look at this new ship. She didn't figure there was anything else to be learned from it. The computer was still sifting through everything she'd scanned at the dreadnought, and that would take a good amount of time.

Even at that, what she had seen of the dreadnought with her eyes looked like the result of a catastrophic encounter with a much larger piece of space junk than she had been hit with. A big ship like that ought to have had energy deflectors to push all but the largest (asteroid sized) pieces of detritus out of the way.

However, hitting something that size would have pulverized the ship and no large pieces would have remained. And even if something that size had been in their path, the ship's nav computer should have sent them around it.

No, she wasn't going to figure this out, and shouldn't be thinking about it anyway. So what if some Free Earthers got themselves blown up? It was nothing to do with her. Those assholes didn't care about her other than as property, so why should she care about them?

● ▪ ▪ ▪ ▬▬▬▬ ▪ ▪ ▬ ııı((◉))ııı ▬ ▪ ▪ ▬▬▬▬ ▪ ▪ ▪ ●

At the same time as the computer was crunching scanner data, keeping the ship from getting destroyed, and monitoring all of the parts of the rig necessary for survival, it was also chewing on how to get the data core unencrypted.

Inez had thrown that in there out of a general curiosity, to see if it could find someone or something that could actually break it down. It wasn't going to help her in the near term, of course. She wasn't going to find out what had hit the dreadnought before getting out of the danger zone.

The rig's computer was nothing especially powerful. The basic architecture of it had been around for over 200 years. It was a workhorse, and it was cheap, which is why it was in ships like hers. Cracking the encryption would take a much newer, more powerful computer than she could get her hands on.

That would mean involving someone else in something that was definitely illegal. Free Earth didn't let their information get out where they couldn't control it, which was another reason that the giant data core was eating at her thoughts.

She also didn't usually cross paths with warships, functioning or otherwise. In fact, she usually picked her jobs out in the middle of nowhere so she could avoid running into the Free Earth as much as possible. Free Earth's very existence had fucked her over enough, she did not want to be anywhere on their scanners.

Technically, she was a citizen of Free Earth, but that had different meanings for different levels of the society. In her case, it let her own property, which was all she cared about. Until ten years ago, she had been property.

Too much of what she was going to be doing over the next two and a half days was just waiting. She had to find something to occupy her mind other than this, or she would go insane. Part of how she survived this long was not thinking about the past. The past was a bad time, while the present and future were okay. Not good, someone like her didn't deserve good (she could hear Sara yelling at her for that), but tolerable.

She'd been going straight out since the rig had been struck. It was probably time to get in her bunk and try to sleep.

Inez was floating in space. She saw the rig getting smaller and smaller as it kept flying, and she was being swallowed up by the immense nothing around her. As far as space was concerned, she was no larger than a pebble, or no smaller than a planet. Space didn't care.

But unlike her panic attack all those years ago, this was comforting. Everyone was equal in the universe's estimation. Equally insignificant. Everyone had just as much impact on whether the universe collapsed or suffered heat death. Brother Lin and Inez just bags of water suspended in space.

She saw Brother Lin, then. The latest leader of Free Earth, wearing the clothes of a laborer, but the unblemished hands of someone who had never worked. His kind eyes the face of the whole thing, but she knew better. His hands held infrasonic blasters, the weapon of choice against people who didn't agree with the Vision. People like Inez.

She spun in space, trying to free herself of the bindings that had her tangled. She shot awake as he pulled the trigger.

Well, part of her dream was accurate. She was floating. She was also tangled up, but in her blankets, not prisoner's robes. She pushed the blankets off of her, and managed to propel herself across the room to a wall panel.

The panel just confirmed what she had suspected. The gravity system had suffered a complete breakdown. This was not going to get fixed before the waystation.

She cursed under her breath, and then had another thought, which had her floating through the short corridors as quickly as she could until she reached the cargo hold. She stopped herself from throwing the door open, but only barely. Explosive decompression would not be a nice way to go.

She turned on the internal surveillance system in the hold, and breathed a sigh of relief. The magnetic flooring was still working. She hadn't lost her cargo. If she was going to be able to afford fixing all of this shit, she absolutely had to deliver this biostock.

She checked the time. She'd managed about five hours in the bunk. She didn't usually do any better than that, so she called that one a win.

On the other hand, five hours was about the longest she'd ever been in Zero-G, so the next two days would be a bit rough. The thing that worried her most were sudden changes in velocity, inertial dampening counted on a certain amount of artificial gravity. A sudden deceleration would very likely turn her into a pile of pudding.

She checked through her systems again, and it looked like she still had enough air for the approximately 40 hours remaining. The gravity system was still drawing power, but not managing to actually use it, which probably meant breaks in the dark matter filaments in the deck plating. That was not going to be cheap.

She had the computer do some calculation, and if she could squeeze a couple of extra hours out of the air, she would be able to do a much gentler deceleration. She would start to slow down with ten hours left, which put her at the right speed for the waystation's autodock (it was advertised as one of the "modern amenities") to catch her.

Once there, safe and sound, she figured she'd send the Company another message. She hoped she could get them to advance her the money to get the rig fixed, but at the very least, they would want to know she had arrived somewhere.

Not for her, she was a replaceable cog, but for the cargo. The cargo was all important.

Not that she hadn't been a good investment for them. After all, they had given her the loan she used to buy the rig, and every payment (including the ridiculous interest) was made on time. Her personal money was in the Company's bank. She had never lost cargo before, and very rarely been late to a delivery.

She was going to be paying off the loan for another 20 years, but it was still better than trying to save up enough to buy the rig outright. That many euan would be nearly impossible for her to scrape together. Ag planets only paid so much and required commitments to stay in one place far longer than she wanted to. She'd have gone insane, or died of a broken liver, far sooner than she would have had more than a small down-payment.

If Zzrft hadn't been so stubborn, she might not have even made it to the end of the year. It really must have loved her, and she felt that guilt again. It had taken her under its wing (well, tentacle) almost from the start. She was barely old enough to qualify to work an ag planet detail, and it was about 400 years old and had worked those sorts of jobs most of its life.

A Grpran like Zzrft could have lived for twice that long, but Zzrft wasn't a lucky Grpran. It'd had a hard life, and must have recognized the same thing in Inez. It was kind, and sarcastic, and an alcoholic, and mostly green except when it was aroused.

Thinking about Zzrft was only going to make her crazy in the here and now. Perhaps it was a good time, though, to start drinking.

The only issue with that was the lack of gravity.
"Fuck."

Inez pulled a ration stick out of her food stores. She
had real food, but much like the booze it would have been far
too messy to try and eat it. Ration bars were her go to when
"Fuck it" was as much as she could muster. Protein, fat,
carbs, nutrients, everything you needed. Other than flavor.
They were a little chewy, and a little powdery, but they were
also of dubious origin. (There was a long running
rumor/joke/conspiracy theory/unhinged rant/hoax that the
meal bars were made from people. On the one hand, she
understood why that theory was popular; on the other, ew.)
Inez usually bought the cheapest ones available, so it was
probably best that they didn't taste like anything.

As she finished the bar, a light on the rig's main
console started blinking. It was a proximity sensor, but it
wasn't picking up scattered debris. It was picking up the
transceiver of an extremely powerful ship. Based on the
readings, it actually wasn't anywhere near her. It was just that
powerful.

She listened to the pulse. Free Earth, a frigate or a
destroyer. Not as big as the dreadnought had been, but still
plenty of firepower. If she pinged back at them, they'd be
able to find her. There was a chance that they would be
friendly. They could almost certainly help her get to port
sooner. Her hand hovered over the signal for ten seconds.
Thirty. Ninety.

"No. Fuck them." She turned off the receiver to remove the temptation.

That was when all the lights on the rig went out.

3

"No, no, no, no."

For about the first minute, her only reaction was blind panic. She couldn't move, let alone do anything about it. The panel lights, the bulkhead lights, everything was out. The engine was still going, she could hear and feel it, and she wasn't dead, which was strong evidence that she hadn't been forced to drop out of faster-than-light speed. Losing FTL without inertial dampening was a one-way ticket to puddingsville. There was no light source, and here that meant absolute blackness.

If the non-drive power was out, that meant that there were many systems that were no longer working. The hull was fairly well insulated, so it shouldn't be losing heat. That didn't stop her from feeling a chill.

The air circulation system would be down. That was the second most immediate concern, after the lights. Without light, fixing anything would be out of the question.

Finally able to make herself move, Inez pushed the cab door open. Without the power assist, and without gravity, it was a harder prospect, but even though it was unusual, the doors were designed to still function in a power failure.

She propelled herself back to her bunk. Part of her wanted to curl up and not come out. She hadn't ever failed at something so hard, especially after years of being pretty good at it. However, as tempting as it was, Inez had a different reason for going there.

She knew the box was under the bed. She just needed to find it. She collided with a bulkhead and hoped the door was the direction she thought it was, as she pulled herself along.

She could smell ozone, which was not great. That usually meant electrical sparking. It also meant system shorts, potential blindness from an unexpected bright light, and oxygen getting repurposed to make something she couldn't damn well breathe.

A couple meters down the bulkhead (she guessed), she found the door. She pulled it open and pulled herself in. She wished she'd thought to set up ropes or a sturdy cable to pull herself along when the gravity went out, but she hadn't expected total fucking darkness, had she? Her bunk cabin was equally dark, and a much smaller space, so the claustrophobic part of her brain she'd been keeping at bay started to nibble at her.

She'd gotten trapped in a small cupboard when she was about four. She was playing, and she didn't know any better. She didn't have a lot of memories about it, other than the fear. Thinking about it now, it was both similar to and the opposite of what she felt in space. The darkness, the blackness, pressed down on her, because she could feel the edges, and not because she couldn't reach the edges, like in space.

Well, she remembered the fear, and the beating the Admiral gave her for being mischievous. But those weren't exactly uncommon. The Admiral was older than her mother by about 40 years. He had a daughter about the same age as Inez and he never laid a hand on her. But Inez was a completely different matter.

She felt around until she found the mattress, which had floated about a half meter above the bunk frame. Below the frame, she could feel boxes. She found one that was about the right shape (based on her memory of when she had stashed it there, four years ago), and carefully opened it.

There were a lot of things in the box. It was full of things she'd taken with her after breaking up with Ihuoma. Since she was only able to see her once every few months, it was probably inevitable. Ihuoma basically gave her an ultimatum, give up the cargo hauling and stay (and live off of her considerable wealth in comfort), or leave and never come back. Inez chose the latter. She still wasn't sure it was the right call.

Her finger looped around a piece of stretchy fabric, and she snatched it. This was it. She wrapped the fabric around her head, closed her eyes, and fingered the switch.

She could tell through her eyelids that the light was working. She put her hand in front of her eyes and slowly opened them. The last thing she wanted was the light shock to blind her and put her out of commission for an hour.

Finally, Inez was able to see without shading her eyes. The light was from excited phosphorescence, so it cast everything in a green glow. That wasn't going to be a huge help if there were colored wires she needed to reattach, but for now it would serve its purpose.

She had bought two of these, one for herself, and one for Ihuoma, during a dumb sightseeing trip to the caverns on Gliese. She didn't know why she'd grabbed it when she was packing her toothbrush and other items, but now she was glad she had.

Inez, now able to see, pushed her way to the exosuit locker. If she ran out of air, this would be her only hope of survival. It had gotten powered up to fifteen hours, so not great, but a good backup. There was no way to run the rig off the exosuit batteries, but going the other way around, she didn't have to worry about using the ship's batteries to power it.

This was making her think of something, just at the corner of her mind, but what that was she couldn't get to coalesce into anything. It was probably just the adrenaline wearing off.

"Focus, Stanton," she chided herself.

Next stop was the aft-most part of the rig, a place she almost never went. It was the home of the ship's drive core, and it unnerved her. It was basically a small, artificial singularity sliding in and out between third and fourth dimension space, generating massive amounts of power as it did so, and all of that power was devoted to propulsion and deflection. It was some smart design that tied the ships debris deflection to the drive. If the deflection was part of main ship's power, if the drive was running and the ship power out (like now), that was a quick way to get done dirty like the dreadnought. Conversely, if your drive died on you (which nearly never happened), you didn't need to worry much about space pebbles hitting you at more than the speed of light.

But you didn't want to spend a lot of time looking at it. The space-time curvature was too much for a brain accustomed to normal, three dimensional things to really process. She'd heard that when they first started to outfit ships with the singularity drives, the engineers almost all went insane within five years. After that, they began recruiting younger and younger for the engineering corps, and then they hit on a solution.

Adult brains, and even adolescent brains, were far too rigid in how they were constructed to be able to process the level of informational input that being near a singularity drive exposed them to, so they got overloaded. The younger a brain was when it was first exposed, the better it was able to withstand the onslaught.

Free Earth started "recruiting" at the age of 3. The families would get a signing bonus, and the children would get full exposure to the singularity for fifteen years. They would never see each other again.

Poor families would sell their children to the butcher shop for scraps of meat, was how Sara put it.

Inez could just make out the door at the other end of the corridor, leading to the singularity. She hoped that with only a little bit of light, she wouldn't be able to see it well enough. She even turned down the light level on her head band before opening the door.

The singularity chamber is a spherical room with a catwalk around the rim. Floating at the center, like a ball of snakes eating their own tails while on fire and frozen at the same time, being laid and hatched and telling you they love you while dying and being reborn as flower skeletons making etchings of their lovers drowning just so, was the singularity. It was its own light and darkness, there and not, twisting through itself and drawing her with a gravity of thought to join with it in eternal oneness but casting her out. There was no railing. It was actually extraordinarily safe, but it did not feel that way.

Inez was here for one reason only, and that was to confirm what she suspected. Crossing the threshold, she felt the pull of gravity again. It only took a quick look at the panels (here they were lit up because of the internal drive power) to show that, no, the power infrastructure could not be bypassed out into the rest of the ship.

The singularity room, and the quantum thrusters that it powered, were a completely different circuit, so that the whole unit could be jettisoned in under a minute. There was literally no way to make it work.

"No, fuck. No, no, fuck, no."

She sank to the floor. There was light and gravity in here, but there was also that thing, being born, fucking, dying and being born again all at once, crumbling away into solidity.

There had to be something else with power. Something she could use to not die. Otherwise, the singularity would keep driving her on without any control. She would run out of Helium-3 in a thousand years but never be able to decelerate. She would go cold, be as frozen as those damn cows in the hold.

She whipped her head up hard enough that she was pretty sure the bulkhead had a dent now.

"Ow, fuck." But she stood up and launched herself back out into the corridor. She did have a source of power. It was there the whole fucking time.

The hold was now entirely airless, and had no gravity, but those electromagnets holding the containers were powered by batteries, not by the ship.

This was going to take some work. Inez flung herself down to the exosuit. It was much harder to put on without gravity to help, and her bushy hair was doing its best to keep the helmet from sealing, but after about half an hour she had it on and was doing pressure checks. Everything was coming up chartreuse, so she turned on the mag boots which gave her stomach a lurch, giving both the illusion of gravity and the sensation of no gravity at the same time.

She was going to have to talk to someone about that. It seemed like a bad design flaw. Like, they could put some dark matter filaments into the insoles to help with that, right? Maybe she would patent that idea, make a mint.

She slowly walked back down the corridor, since the mag boots had to latch and unlatch with every step. She opened the inner door, stepped in, and closed the door behind her. The space between the inner and outer doors was just about coffin sized, but at least there was a window.

She manually checked to make sure no air was making it past the door, and raised the helmet. She turned to the outer door, and spun the latch mechanism. It used an old-style physical latch and strong polymer gasket to achieve air-tightness, so it was a bit tough to turn without the power assist, but she managed.

There were twenty-four crates, each with massively powerful batteries running two systems. One system was keeping the crates in place magnetically. The other was keeping the cattle alive in suspension.

She'd done enough thumbnail electrical calculations to know she would need a whole battery's worth of power. However, if she put them into series, then it would only take one 24th from each, and she wouldn't lose her cargo or her life.

She was going to need some heavy cables, which most detachable cargo holds had in a storage compartment somewhere. If she was lucky, it wasn't at the end with the giant hole. She saw faintly a diagram painted on a sheet of metal next to the door, and aimed her exosuit light on it. A small stick figure at one end of the 500 meter long hold showed where she was. She looked along the edges of the map, but there was nothing that looked like a storage room. No rooms at all.

She hit the stanchion it was attached to a few times, before remembering that it was painted and not a screen, and screens didn't much like being hit anyway.

Hitting it caused some corrosion to fall away, though, and she saw a little X pretty much in the center of the hold. Of course, it was under the deck plating. The mag boots and lack of gravity should allow her to raise the doorway without assistance, but she wasn't positive.

She was already further into a cargo hold than she usually went, and she was going to have to walk straight down the middle toward the giant hole, with it looking like stars were right there. She knew they were going three and a half thousand times the speed of light, and right now that was not a comforting thought either.

Inez worked her way down to the spot the X had marked. It was a magnetically sealed polymerized plate, so not as heavy (no, massive) as a typical deck plate. She just needed to pop open the magnets and the rest should be easy. Since it wasn't uncommon for the cargo holds to be without power, there was a very convenient lever embedded in the floor, which she pulled.

She heard the vibration of the magnets disengaging coming up from her feet in a muffled thump. She looped her fingers into the release handle and a mechanical hydraulic arm lifted it up. This was getting to be too easy. It was almost like they had her sort of catastrophe in mind at some point.

She found the heavy cables she needed, about 2 km of 5 mm bundled superconductive carbon nanotube. She also found a hole punch, epoxy, connector clamps, and heavy clippers. She attached all of that to the exosuit's utility belt, grabbed the spool of cable, and went back up to the cargo deck. She shut the bulkhead door behind her, to make sure nothing that was loose got any ideas about going anywhere.

Now she really did need to go out under the giant hole in the roof. She was magnetically attached to the deck plating, and inertia alone would keep her from floating out, but damn it was not good. The edges were much more jagged up in person, and having something under your feet didn't make having nothing overhead any better.

"So don't look up, asshole," she muttered, and focused on getting to the last one on her right. Head down, she could tell that the containers would have their batteries along the back, well, outer sides, of the crates. Each crate was 20 meters apart, and 20 meters wide. They were also about 60 meters long and 10 meters tall. This was a fairly standard size for suspended farm animals. Each one could house up to 3,000, and this shipment would probably be enough for an entire colony world of several million people.

Assuming it was bovine. If it was sheep, goats or swine, it could be even more. All it said was biostock, which could mean virtually anything, but cattle was the most likely.

Great, millions of people's lives possibly hanging in the balance. That was the last thought she needed in her head right now.

She found the panel on the back side of the last crate and pressed the button to open it. She was grateful that it still had power, since this whole thing would be moot if it was dead. The battery had more than 75% of its power left. Excellent. She stuck the end of the cable into the clamp and felt it snap into place. Then she clamped it to the output lead and felt that click.

She moved down the line, cutting the cable, clamping it to the input, clamping the next section of cable to the output, until she got back up to the rear of the hold. Then she repeated it on the other side. It took the better part of three hours to get everything hooked up in a series, with the two cables from each side coming together about ten meters from the door.

She saw a flash from the back of the nearest one to her on the left. That was the last one she'd hooked up, and a flash like that was not good news. She rushed over as fast as she was able, and saw that the battery had ejected part of its storage medium. As far a she could tell, it still had about 50% of its power, and it should still be able to function how she needed, but she would have to make sure she kept an eye on these.

She also had to make sure that the overload hadn't fried the suspension systems, since that would mean this crate's contents would all be dead, and in this case it would be completely her fault. That meant going back around to the front of the crate.

Just like on the back, there wasn't any outward sign of what was inside, just a "Property of the Free Earth" stencil and a number, as well as an arrow pointing to the latch saying "Open Here".

The latch was pretty stubborn, though, and this took more effort than she had expected. She changed her angle by climbing up the side of the crate until she was looking down at the latch, dug in her magnetic heels and pulled as hard as she could.

The latch finally gave way, and Inez again reoriented herself and pulled the door open. Closing it again would be easy, as it had an auto close. Why they didn't also put an auto open on it, she figured had to do with deterring people from doing exactly what she was doing now.

The first thing she saw was the panel glowing on the inside of the door. It had everything showing nominal, so it looked like she had lucked out entirely. Everything in this crate was still alive. 18,000 units. Damn, that's a big number. It must be something a lot smaller than cattle.

"Oh, shit. No." She spun away, with an empty chasm forming in her gut. Then she turned back. She had to know.

She turned on the internal observation camera. Staring back at her was the sad pale face of an 8 year old boy.

4

Thirty-one years ago, when she was 15, Pamela Stanton's family sold her into bondage. They were very poor, needed money to stay alive and thought it was better for her than death. She ended up in the household of Admiral Cotton Ringwald. The man was in his prime, sixty-three Earth years old, and commander of the two fleets controlling the colonies on the inner side of the Orion Arm.

She quickly rose up in the household staff, becoming the personal cook for the Admiral himself. This was partly because she knew how to cook, which most of the other slaves did not, and partly because she was young and beautiful, and the Admiral was not shy about expressing his attraction to her.

After three years, Pamela gave in just once, hoping that it would stop the constant glances and comments. The man disgusted her. Unfortunately, it only made things worse, as his wife and Pamela both became pregnant around the same time. (The Admiral's wife, not much older than Pamela herself, clearly hated the man, but hated Pamela even more.)

Pamela had tried more than once to get drugs to end it, but had been caught each time. Eventually she was put under guard until she gave birth. Inez was born, and by the laws of the time, was immediately made property of the household. (Some of this Pamela had told her, but much of it had to be gleaned from what people around her said and didn't say.) The Admiral's wife also had a daughter, a free girl, named Sara, and the two were raised together. Pamela's job was changed from cook to nursemaid, and so she spent hours each day with both girls. At night, she would give Sara to her mother to be in the Admiral's quarters, and take Inez down to the dirty closet that she had for sleeping.

As slave children went, Inez was treated reasonably well. Sara was like a sister to her, though early on Inez understood the reality of their two situations. By the time she was five, she had already been put to work in the kitchen. Meanwhile, her mother, who was now teaching Sara her numbers and words, would spend precious sleep hours teaching Inez. She didn't want her daughter growing up unable to defend herself, so she also drilled into her theory about politics and weapons, in case she ever needed them.

The Admiral killed Pamela Stanton when Inez was 11. It wasn't because of anything she had done to upset him. They were both very careful, but there were times when someone who was cruel would be cruel for no reason. That's another lesson Inez learned early.

Inez was sleeping next to her mother when the Admiral visited them, as he did whenever he wasn't out with his fleet. He climbed on top of Pamela and started trying to rape her, but he was unable to get an erection. He started choking her then, hoping it would fix his issue. He kept choking until she was unable to breathe ever again. Inez kept completely still. She knew what was happening, and she couldn't do anything.

Killing a slave was not a crime, just a business loss, so Pamela's body was vaporized. Inez was left to keep working for this household, but she was moved out to the mechanic bay so that the Admiral's wife wouldn't need to see this reminder of what her husband was.

Out with the older men of the maintenance crew, she learned how to take care of engines and other systems.

This whole history was always right under the surface of who Inez was. No matter how hard she tried to move past it, to understand that in the end, she was the victor and the Admiral was not even dust, it was still there.

And now, seeing this boy, understanding just how many of these people there were, this was... well, she didn't know what it was, but it wasn't good.

Based on the exosuit's clock, she'd been staring at the screen for at least ten minutes.

"Goddammit," she said, finally, and shut the crate's door. She finished reconnecting this crate to the rest of her repairs, and then fed a lead to the door. She used the hole punch to make a hole that would take the cable, and fed it through. She made sure there was enough slack, and then pulled out the epoxy gun to seal around the cable.

Back in the rig, she connected the cable to the internal power, and the lights came back up. Out of an excess of caution and not wanting to kill the people in the hold (fucking people), she turned out all but the most minimal lights and powered systems, and headed back to the cab.

● ▪ ▪ ▪ ━━━━ ▪▪ ▪ ━ ıı((◉))ıı ━ ▪▪ ▪ ━━━━ ▪ ▪ ▪ ●

The fucking Free Earth. Most of the colonies founded in the last hundred years were trying to escape Free Earth control, but ended up under their thumb anyway. Outwardly, they gave the appearance of democracy and representation, but that was only for the top 5%. Everyone else was a slave, either in fact or in effect.

When she had broken free, she had no idea what to do with herself. She had just enough euan to get off the planet, but then what? After sleeping on benches for a few nights on the planet's emigration station, she saw an ad for ag-planet supervisors, no experience needed, and signed on.

Two trillion and some-odd residents of the Free Earth, and over 90% of them had never even seen Earth. Inez certainly hadn't. It held no allure for her. Even if it was the paradise that they made it out to be, it was built on the work of people like her. She may have escaped slavery, but she would never escape the work.

Her mother hadn't given her a lot of ancient history lessons, but she'd figured out that before the Free Earth, there was the Terran Empire, and before that, the Terran Confederation and the Outer Colonies. Slavery had crept in then, as indentured servitude first, and then the slippery slope was fast and steep. Pamela and Inez were hardly unique.

And now, she was carrying a hold full of people just like her.

She wished, not for the first time, that Sara was there. Sara wasn't like the Admiral and his wife. She grew up in luxury, but understood what it cost. She had a clear head about these things, and since she was 16 at the time, had been the one to legally emancipate Inez following her father's "disappearance".

But a first love wasn't going to have the solution for her now.

The choices were horrible. Every choice she could make would be the worst choice.

She could set the slaves free. She wanted to set the slaves free. Where to set them free, though. They could start a colony, but locating worlds that weren't already colonized or in need of terraforming would be nearly impossible. That life might actually be worse than slavery, except that they would be free.

Though, each one would have a biochip under their sternum, placed specifically to keep it from being easy to remove, and which would tip off any scanners at any ports that they were escaped slaves.

She didn't know their stories. Were these people who sold themselves into slavery? Not the children, of course, but the rest of them? Undoubtedly some of them were, and if they didn't show up where they were supposed to, the people they were trying to help would not get paid. Insurance would pay the owners for lost property, but nothing covered those who were desperate enough to do this.

Could she go to a non-governmental organization? There were anti-slavery organizations, like Freedom Fleet, but most of them were seen as cranks and terrorists and not a real political force. Still, that was a possibility.

Anything she did to "lose" her cargo, though, would mark her as a criminal. The lowest level would just be losing through no action of her own. In other words, if the debris strike had actually destroyed the hold, and they could recover the bodies, she would be charged with negligence and serve a year on a low security prison world. If they were not able to recover the bodies, that would be property destruction, which was five years in medium security.

If they caught her freeing the slaves, that was life in supermax, or even vaporization.

Virtually anything she did to try and improve these people's future lives would probably backfire and cause her to be imprisoned for the rest of her life.

So what was the other choice, delivering them? Letting them suffer worse than she had suffered?

These were not choices, just a continuum of fucking terrible.

● - - - ▬▬▬▬ - - - ▬ ιι((◉))ιι ▬ - - - ▬▬▬▬ - - - ●

Inez was not hungry, but it had been six hours since she'd eaten anything, so she got out a meal bar and took little bites. There still wasn't any gravity, that would take more than power to fix, but there were lights and the cab had all of its panels working. The central computer had taken about ten minutes to reboot, and when it did, she saw that there was a message for her.

It was the Company, which was not owned by the Free Earth, but it was incorporated there, so it ran under their laws. She couldn't even run this by them. They probably knew what her cargo was, and didn't care.

This message was in response to her initial note to them about the collision. Her assignment manager, a woman that Inez had only met once, and only had real-time conversations with about ten times in the last seven years, was the one who had finally gotten back to her. She knew that her comms system was working well enough that messages should only take an hour to get back to her office, so the fact that it both merited a response and took a whole day to do so was odd.

Her original message to them was fairly straightforward, talking about the hit and her plan to go to the waystation. She hadn't informed them about any of the other things, like the dreadnought and the data cube. She hadn't even had a chance to tell them about losing power yet.

"IS:

"Glad you aren't hurt. Please take care with cargo. This is an extremely valuable haul for you. Given the trouble you are having, safe delivery of the cargo is carrying a 2,000 euan bonus on this, without a timeliness requirement.

"HU."

Two thousand euan. Over the last seven years, she had only paid off about 500 euan on the rig. Two thousand, that was freedom. Just one thousand would pay off the rig. Her loan covering the rig was with the company, so they knew what she was worth.

That was a hell of a turn of phrase. She wanted to punch the wall, but managed to stop herself. A broken hand on top of everything else would be a bad idea.

"Every goddamn thing is a bad idea," she yelled as loud as she could.

Trading these people's lives for her own freedom--a bad idea. But freeing them and trying to make a run for it-- also a bad idea. These people should be allowed their freedom, but the cost was staggering. Even more so now.

Inez felt like she was going to vomit (another bad idea in zero-g). She had to force herself to stop thinking about it.

She decided on the most brainless activity she could think of, that old Russian block game.

Stacking the falling blocks, completing lines across to make blocks disappear, fitting the shapes together. This made sense. This had a logical progression. As the speed of the falling blocks increased, she had to concentrate on moving and rotating them without time to consciously decide where they were going. She hadn't played in a long time, so it took a few rounds to get back into the flow, but it was a lot like flying. Once you knew how, it was almost impossible to forget.

She was sitting in the cab with the holographic display of the bricks falling, her partly eaten meal bar long forgotten, playing as though her entire life depended on doing nothing but playing this game.

The console beeping at her nearly gave her a heart attack. She pushed the game away and pulled up the reason for the sudden noise.

It was more debris. The rig was avoiding it now, with ease, but she was getting good at recognizing ship debris from a distance. This was mostly clustered about three kilometers from her current position, with a few items out her way as well. It was the clustering that really gave away that it was a ship. Still, given the general shape of the rig, stopping for a look would be a terrible idea.

Another terrible idea.

She could hear Ihuoma in her head, in her lilting accent and deep alto, "You got yourself backed into a corner. You can't fix everything."

She'd said that many times. She was a good woman, and Inez was somewhere other than good. Sure, it was due to circumstance, but she still had blood on her hands. Ihuoma knew that, and loved her anyway. Ihuoma was a god damned princess, literally. She was heir to the seat of power on her colony, one of the old colonies that wasn't so beholden to the Free Earth.

More often than not, what Ihuoma meant was "Don't get yourself killed," or "Don't do something stupid and die." Even after Inez left, Ihuoma had sent her a message, not angry or sad, but resigned. "You got yourself backed into a corner, kyau daya. You can't fix it all."

"I can't fix it all. I can fix something."

Don't get yourself killed, fix something.

She repeated this to herself a few times. Deep breaths. A few more times. This was not going to overtake her.

"You can't fix anything if you're dead."

Inez checked the time, and she still had a full day before reaching the waystation. She'd managed through two terrible days and a half-dozen panic attacks at that point, which she honestly felt was a lower number than the situation warranted.

She was settled in her seat at the ship's console, trying to will the time to pass. More, that it should pass without any further shocks to her system or the ship's. She wasn't sure either of them would survive if one more thing happened.

She still hadn't responded to the message from the Company. It wasn't like she had to accept the offer, it was part of her contract, but she should let them know that she was, in fact, still alive and capable of carrying out the task. But acknowledging it without revealing she'd looked in the crates, that was the hard part.

Of course they knew that she had slaves on her ship. It's not like slavery was a closely guarded secret. It wasn't publicized (did they, perhaps, know shame?), but it was completely legal and even expected.

How many runs had she done? How many crates of "biostock" had she delivered? How many slaves had she condemned to lives worse than her own? At least she had gotten free. After the Admiral's "disappearance", his will said that Sara got everything, while his wife got nothing. If she'd been younger, an executor would have been appointed and Inez would probably never have gotten away.

That also would have probably resulted in finding the real will in the household's computers, but Sara was really good at her work.

Damn. If she was going to get that cube decoded, Sara would probably have to be involved. Not that the data cube was top of mind right now, but it still didn't make any sense. A dreadnought out on this lane didn't make a whole lot of sense to begin with, since this was Free Earth loyalist territory for the most part. Dreadnoughts mostly got used to keep less stable systems from thinking about breaking away, or to fight in their war (thirty years of stalemate and counting) with the Hand of the Gods.

The Hand of the Gods wasn't their real name. No one knew their real name. They'd shown up at the edges of Earth space five decades before, and refused contact. If their ships were defeated, then they would obliterate themselves rather than be captured. They were called the Hand of the Gods because after they attacked a colony for the first time, press reports quoted a Marine general saying it has been turned to ash by the hand of the Gods, and the press loves a good nickname.

If Free Earth intelligence knew anything about them, they weren't telling the public. But that was on the other side of the Orion arm, so she figured there wasn't some super-weapon that the Hand had developed. She wasn't going to find the evidence of one out here, let alone a dreadnought that they'd pulverized.

(Hmm. Thinking about this was good. Thinking about this meant she wasn't thinking about the other thing.)

Alright, the scans hadn't shown any sort of weapons fire or plasma burns or anything. If it was the Hand, then they had somehow caused its instant destruction and the near instant death of the whole crew. They had also kept the beacon from launching, which would have been ready to go as soon as an enemy ship appeared. So if they had been attacked, whatever it was either showed up and took them out in the same instant, or the dreadnought thought they were friendly.

This was making her head spin a bit, with the possibilities. The sudden deceleration that would be required for the first option was the stuff of science fiction. They needed to come down to a slower speed before they could think of stopping, otherwise they would be dead. Even computer circuits couldn't get through it unscathed, and biological organisms were another matter entirely.

The deceleration takes about five minutes, during which time they would have been detected. Even if the Hand were an artificial sentience (again, the realm of science fiction), any less time than that and they could not have enough inertial dampening to avoid scrambling their components and being rendered inert.

But the second option, were they masquerading as a Free Earth ship? A trader vessel? A rig? Or were they flying under a flag of truce, only to attack when they got inside the defenses?

Inez now really wanted to get the cube decoded. Her scans didn't indicate that there had been any other ship, but that had its own set of questions. Was it hit by space debris, like she was? It was clearly near stopped when it was hit, based on the bodies she found being largely whole. If it had hit a space rock at speed, the bodies would be mostly jelly.

That meant whatever hit them was going fast. Maybe 30% of the speed of light. And it would have been small. They would have to have not seen it coming (including the automatic deflector systems that were always looking for dangers).

But how a pebble (no bigger than the top digit on her pinkie) could get up to that sort of speed, that was outside of what she knew.

Inez started seeing the local pings from the waystation on the console, and she pinged back, letting them know she was incoming and in need of repairs. It was always a good idea to warn them when you were only flying pieces of a ship so they could be ready for you.

After her reply was sent, she almost immediately got a comms request. She quickly checked her hair, then remembered there was nothing she could do about it, and opened the channel.

A young east Asian man with bright eyes and hair pulled back into what looked like a long braid appeared in front of her.

"Rig 882A5NH95D, this is waystation Zìyóu dìqiú zāo tòule. You are in need of assistance?"

"It is nice to hear another voice, waystation Zìyóu dìqiú zāo tòule." Free Earth Sucks. Nice. "This is Rig 882A5NH95D, or Inez to my friends."

"Hymie Fang, at your service." He bowed slightly, in what was clearly an act. There was a Sino-nostalgia movement that had gone on for a decade now, but mostly it used old stereotypes of subservience for inspiration. Vids from the 20th century were the most popular source of material for them, and so lots of people with Asian looks played along to get their tips.

"So, I was hit by some debris about two days ago, which has caused a number of system issues and also ripped the upper front bulkhead off my cargo hold. I'm going to need some patches."

The act dropped as Inez described the damage. "Damn, girl. How are you still alive?"

"It's just my bad luck streak. I'm going to initiate deceleration in five hours, so you should be able to catch me with your autodock."

A troubled look came across Hymie's face. He bit his upper lip for a second, before catching himself.

Inez sighed. "Alright. What's wrong with the autodock?"

5

"You have to understand, most of the ships that come here just use the autodock as a convenience. They aren't--"

"About to crumble into dust?"

The young station attendant looked like he might actually start crying. "About a month ago, the transmission arm of the autodock was shorn clear off the rest of it. Something must have hit it, but we didn't see anything. It just stopped sending out the grappler signal. Since then, we just haven't been able to get someone here to fix it. The mechanotrons don't have the programming."

Inez wasn't really listening. In her head, she was doing calculations. Without the auto-dock, she would need to decelerate sooner, and for longer, in order to be at a speed where she could manage docking herself. The auto-dock could grab hold of a ship going one percent of light speed, or about 3000 km per second. In order for her to dock on her own, she would need to be at one percent of that, or 30km per second.

Even going that fast, she would have to slam on the brakes when she got to the waystation, without the auto-doc providing any mitigation of the inertia.

She had already planned the gentle deceleration path, but this was going to have to be a lot less gentle.

The rig would decelerate basically in the old fashioned way. Right now, she was coasting on inertia. She would need to swing the rig 180 degrees to put the thrusters in front of her, and then push the power up over several hours.

There were two kinds of motion that the drive employed. There was force propulsion, and there was bend propulsion. It used both simultaneously to allow faster than light travel that avoided the time dilation caused by relativity.

Somehow. She had gotten a bit lost when she tried to teach it to herself.

At any rate, the turn was going to need to happen now.

"Waystation, I am beginning decel op now. Decel will take fifteen hours."

Hymie looked very concerned now. "Two problems with that. One, you're going to experience a lot of inertial force. The other, your read out here says that you only have ten hours of breathable air."

"One way or another, I may die. At least this way, I won't be floating out in space forever."

"I read you, Inez. Good luck. We'll be waiting for you here."

● ● ● ● ▬▬▬▬ ● ● ▬ ıı((◉))ıı ▬ ● ● ▬▬▬▬ ● ● ● ●

Inez checked the ship's orientation. It was right on for deceleration trajectory. "Don't die," she whispered to herself, and executed the start of deceleration. She didn't really feel much at first, but that was a good thing. She was concerned about how much she was going to be feeling very soon. Even with working inertial dampening, which she was pretty sure she didn't have, moving around in the ship was going to get difficult within an hour. She figured she had maybe three quarters of that before she wouldn't be able to do much of anything.

She pushed herself down the corridor to her exosuit. Three times in three days she'd pulled this on without any decontamination, and it was staring to smell ripe. She checked the air reserves, which had about three hours worth now. So, when she did run out of air, she was somehow going to need to make three hours last for five.

If she filled the tank from the ship's air supply, the air wouldn't need to fill as large a space, and might last longer. She checked the time, and the decel was fifteen minutes in. She would have to be quick about this.

She turned off the mag boots and drifted toward the cargo hold. There was clearly some inertia going on now. She fought against it and found the small cupboard where the air circulator was housed. She unclasped the hose for her suit air and attached it to the ship's air. Twenty minutes to go. Twenty minutes and she probably wouldn't be able to get back to the cab.

Inez turned up the flow of air into the suit, and the suit was capturing what it needed and discarding the rest. This suit was much smarter than anything else she owned, and it knew higher oxygen and lower nitrogen in the mix would be needed. The glowing dial on the suit's readout was showing the climb in breathing time. Six hours now. She just wasn't sure how much it was costing.

Ten minutes to go, and seven hours in the tank. She was not going to make this. "Come on, bastard. Come on."

Five minutes, ten hours. She needed more. She reactivated the mag boots because she could feel the pull of inertia kicking in now. With the mag boots assisting, maybe she could get a couple more minutes out of it. Minutes meant hours.

Three minutes, twelve hours. Inez slapped the helmet into place in the suit, which automatically increased the air pressure against her face. The pressure outside of the suit had been noticeably lower, so it was probably a good time to do that.

One minute, fourteen hours. Just over fourteen hours between her and the waystation. She needed that last minute.

Her clock flashed in her vision. Time. She checked the tank, and she had fourteen and a half hours. Now she had to get to the cab against the momentum. The rig was basically a triangle. Along one edge was the cargo hold, and at the point across from it was the drive and the thrusters. Looking forward (which was now backward, with having turned around), to the right was the storage room where the exosuit was kept, and then through there was one of the doors to the cab.

It was like trying to walk through rye fields on the ag planet after one of the torrential rains that happened a few times a month. Each step sticking because of the mag boots, forward motion slowed by the nearly lateral force from deceleration. She could still see the countdown clock, watching the minutes tick away as she walked the ten meters to the open door of the cab.

"Fucking motherfucker," she grumbled, with effort. She felt like Zeno's paradox was mocking her, that she would never get all the way, just always managing half.

Slowly, though, the distance was vanishing. The clock saying she'd spent fifteen minutes so far just trying to walk. She was going to need to recommend this as the next exercise trend. It had to be burning a ton of calories. Now she regretted not finishing her meal bar. Well, it probably wasn't going to matter much soon.

Another twenty minutes and she could reach the doorway. She used her arms to steady herself and took a much longer step. Inside the cab. Just need the chair. Then she was in front of the chair, and allowed the momentum to pull her into it.

The thrusters would be increasing their output for another two hours, maintaining for two, and then slowly backing off. With only the limited inertial dampening, the worst would be the drop to sub-light speed. She had stopped before, but that was with full gravity and inertial protection, which made fast-stop maneuvers non-fatal.

There was a dilation effect both entering and exiting faster-than-light speeds. It presented itself as microseconds of high gravitation. Early test pilots called it the light boom, but Inez always thought of it as instant space sickness. She'd gotten through it just fine in the past, but there was a non-zero chance that she might throw up in her suit while her inner ears were completely out of alignment. Maybe it was good she hadn't eaten much.

That moment would be coming five hours before reaching the waystation. She had, according to her suit clock, about seven hours before then. And assuming everything went well, she would then have to wake up her overworked body and actually dock on her own, something she'd only ever done twice. And those times, the rig was working. And she hadn't had thousands of slaves in her hold then.

This wasn't going away, any part of it. She had managed to go for a few hours without her brain's circular firing squad making a nuisance, but now she had hours where literally all there was to do was think.

Zzrft was right. She wanted to be the tough loner, and she could do it if she could keep distracted, and if nothing else interfered with her desire to stay out of it all. She wasn't a hero, she was just a cargoist. And it hurt knowing that.

Those slaves didn't know who she was, but they were counting on her to keep them as safe as she could. That boy (god, how many of them were children?) needed her to keep her head on straight so that he could maybe grow up and, what? Lead a rebellion? Follow the same muck-encrusted path that she had? Face the same impossible choice?

When their year on the ag planet was up, Zzrft signed on for another year. That was the work it was used to, and it even liked it up to a point. Humans were hard for it to figure out, since they didn't change color to show feelings and only had one hole for speaking and eating. Two or three at a time was much easier. But Inez was off to try and make this thing work.

It wasn't until after they had no way to be in touch anymore that she realized it had deposited its year's earnings in her account. She was indebted to Zzrft in a way that she owed no other being. Sara had given her freedom, Ihuoma had given her love. But Zzrft had given her a chance at her own life, damn them. She couldn't just throw that away.

She'd never really noticed how her chair would face backwards when decelerating before. The rig didn't have windows out onto space, since sensors were much more useful than visual input. (Things in space always looked much smaller than they were, without context or scale.) Now, though, she kind of wanted to see the blueshift lessen.

Alone with her thoughts and nothing to occupy her. This was the nightmare that Zzrft had mentioned. At 17, that sounded like heaven. In actuality, this was torture. She felt tears streaking back from her eyes, and she honestly didn't know if it was from the pain she was feeling or the heartache.

Because she knew. Of course she knew what she was going to do. What she would have to do. She knew as soon as she'd seen his face, so innocent, his eyes shut like he was sleeping. She knew what those eyes would look like when he woke up. His flat nose and short, kinky hair and his ribs visible in his chest. She had seen him so many times before, and she was going to see him many times again.

Gods, they shipped them naked. They probably justified it by the weight of clothing or some other bullshit, but she knew what it was. It was a reminder of their status. That dignity was not something they were afforded. They would never be human again. She was sure she would see on all of the shoulders the same thing that used to be on her own, the Free Earth logo and a scan line. The same thing that would be on the rump of all of the cattle. They were property. A commodity.

The message from the Company was displayed in front of her. She leaned forward as much as she could, and typed her reply.

Five hours to go, and she was about to go sub-light. It was some time now since she'd been able to move at all. The chair was made to provide protection from inertial forces in the case of failures, but this was probably past what was intended for it. Once the rig was going less than 300,000 km per second, the forces should let up a bit, steadily decreasing as she approached the waystation.

That was important, since if she was going to pilot the rig into the waystation, she would need to be able to move.

Her eyeballs hurt in ways she had never considered before. Her hair hurt. She had an itch on her nose that had come and gone for the last hour. She somehow managed to stay conscious through this, even though she couldn't keep her eyes open for long. Even when they were open, she couldn't focus on anything. The batteries were still connected, which was good. If the rig lost power at this point, the deceleration program would keep running, and she would end up accelerating in the opposite direction.

Through the display in her exosuit helmet, she could see that the rig was still on track. Enough had gone right with this that she was actually more nervous than at the start. The way this trip had gone, there was no way she was going to assume a span of good luck would last.

The ship lurched, and the chipper voice of the computer said, "Mae'r cyflymder bellach yn llai na dau gant wyth deg mil o gilometrau yr eiliad." That was it. Even not understanding a single word, she knew. Sub-light speed. Now if something hit, she would simply be blown up and not atomized.

Now there was a point. Whatever had hit the Free Earth ship couldn't have been traveling faster than light, nor could the ship itself, or the level of energy involved would have rendered both down to the atomic (or even sub-atomic) level. She wouldn't have found anything. Two ships traveling faster than light colliding (a glancing blow, not even head-on) had produced enough energy to destroy an entire fleet at the Battle of Polaris Sigma, one of the stories her mother had taught her when she was a child.

Before the Hands, before even Free Earth, the Terran Empire flew around explored space to make sure that no colonies got any ideas about freeing themselves. They lacked real-time communication between ships, and accidents weren't uncommon.

In this case, though, they were hunting down dissidents, and those dissidents got wind they were coming. Their leader dropped everyone off the frigate that they had stolen, and then sped to meet the incoming fleet. Seeing that they were incoming faster than light, the leader aimed for where the most central ship would be, and went to light speed. The ships hit at an angle, and a bit off plane, but it was more than enough to turn both ships into particles traveling the speed of light, which radiated out and hit the other ships in the fleet.

Of twelve ships, only two remained intact, but with severe damage. One was captured by the dissidents, and the other was able to limp back to the Empire. That ship carried Xavier Burkus, who in turn led a rebellion against the Empire, and become Brother Xavier of the Free Earth.

So whatever hit the ship was not past the light barrier, and neither was the ship itself. Her own rig was in a light-speed cool-down when it was hit (these are recommended every twelve hours, but that wasn't something she had worried about so much since the hit).

It still didn't make any sense. Lower than light speed, a ship like a dreadnought would be able to detect something else coming in at less than light speed in enough time to make the adjustment and avoid it.

The computer chirped. Four hours to go.

● ■ ■ ■ ▬▬▬▬▬ ■ ■ ▬ ιι((◉))ιι ▬ ■ ■ ▬▬▬▬▬ ■ ■ ■ ●

A message popped up on the display. "Anomaly detected in data." Data? What data was this about?

Inez reached out toward it, and was surprised how easy it was. Clearly the inertia was really letting up. Her gloved finger tapped it, and the message opened up.

"Anomaly detected in data. Biological material in ship debris 50% higher than expected for dreadnought class ship."

She had completely forgotten about the computer crunching the dreadnought data, and was honestly surprised that it was still being analyzed. After all, the computer had needed to be rebooted after the power was re-established, and she didn't think she had told it to do that.

It was carrying extra people. A lot of extra people. The standard crew was around 950, so nearly 500 more people (or a whole lot of fat crewmembers, which seemed unlikely). Nothing about this was adding up.

The computer chirped again. Fifteen minutes until she needed to take over control. She pressed the manual control button, which opened a panel under the console, and a stick control for manual piloting rose up in front of her.

She hadn't been trained as a pilot, but she had learned a lot in the last several years and she wasn't bad at it. At least, she had never crashed. She'd think she had a lucky streak, except for every other thing in her life right now.

It was designed for human hands, but probably for male hands. The finger slots felt just a hair too far apart. Not that she wasn't accustomed to using things made for men, but it still wasn't comfortable.

She was now slowed down to about 30 km per second, and dropping. She goosed up the throttle to make it slow more quickly, and a dot on the display showed her where the waystation was. It was orbiting a small rocky planet that didn't have an atmosphere, and had once been used for mining a wide variety of resources. It was stripped until there was almost nothing left but base rock. She could actually see the planet, though not well. The waystation would have been invisible without the dot.

10 kilometers per second. Eight. Five. Two. The waystation was now ping-pong ball sized, and she nudged herself into a direct approach. 0.3 kilometers per second. This was the speed where the autodock would have picked her up if it was working. 0.05 km, or 50 meters per second. The

waystation filled half the display, and she could see the docking lights telling her where to go.

That's when she saw her mistake. There were three other ships at the docking ring. Two belonged to the Company, in their trademark brown with the gold shield logo on the side. The third was Free Earth military.

"Shiiiiit," came out of her, barely a breath.

She froze, just for a second, but it was long enough to throw it all off. She pushed the thrusters to full, yanked the stick to the left, but nothing she did at that point could stop the rig from hitting the docking port.

Inez registered the lights going out as she was catapulted backward from her seat. Then she hit the bulkhead and passed out.

6

The room was bright. It took a few minutes for Inez to adjust to just how bright it was. Her head felt like her hangover had a hangover. There was a definite antiseptic smell in the air, which didn't help her head. On the other hand it was quiet. Blessedly quiet. Should it be that quiet?

Once she was able to keep her eyes open for more than a minute at a time, she was able to focus on objects. The walls and ceiling were white, and very brightly lit. She was lying down on a skinny mattress, and there was an iv tube attached to her arm. She wasn't dead, unless this was some weird purgatory thing.

She must have been recovered from the rig. This was a well appointed medical suite, but she was the only person in this room. It was probably on the waystation, and not on one of the other ships. The Company would probably have a medic, and Free Earth would have at least two doctors and a half dozen nurses buzzing around. Waystations, especially ones like this that are off the main routes, are typically run by a minimal staff and lots of automatons. The "doctor" here was probably an old medic-bot.

She pushed herself up to a sitting position, and the room responded by spinning uncontrollably for a minute. She could smell the bile rising in her throat, but managed to push it back down again. Her body had re-acclimated to gravity while she was out, at least.

"Doc?" she called to the room. Her voice was hoarse, and again she wondered how long it had been since she'd spoken.

A small, white box trundled over to her almost silently. There was a red X on the side, indicating it was a medic. The top split open and a telescoping arm rose out of it. At the end of the arm was a sensor package. Someone had painted a name onto it, "Hu, MD." "What's wrong with me?"

"Three broken ribs. Concussion. Numerous contusions, sprains. Lung damage from oxygen starvation." Ribs and lungs. No wonder her chest was sore. She ran her hand along the sharpest feeling pain spots.

"How long have I been under?"

"Twelve hours. Lungs have been repaired, bones are fusing. Recommend remaining in repose."

Half a day? Well, that was plenty of time for everything to fall apart. "Do you know what shape my rig is in?"

It looked like it tilted its sensor package to the side. "Accessing. Mechanotrons are working on internal systems. Gravity systems at 53% completed. Electrical systems 27% completed. Hull fully repaired." The medic-bot had a flat, genderless voice that was supposed to be comforting, but ended up sounding much more disinterested.

At least one of them would be able to move soon. "How many people are on this station?"

"One."

"Wait, Fang is the only one here?"

"Negative."

What did that-- "Oh, god. The one is me?"

"Affirmative."

"Are the other ships still docked?"

"One ship remains docked, registered 'The Tenth Great and Glorious Browns Company #CS89091'. Zero crew is on board."

What the hell? "Doc, I need to know what happened. Can you leave this medbay?"

"Affirmative."

"Alright. I need you to lead me to the control deck."

"Negative."

"What? I'm human, you have to obey my orders."

"First do no harm. Allowing you to leave this medbay would cause irreparable damage to you. This takes precedence over following orders." Inez didn't deal with automatons very often, and wasn't entirely sure what to do here.

"Doc, I need to get to the control deck so I can find out what happened here. Why I'm still here."

The sensor package tilted again. It must have been programmed to appear like it was thinking. This, at least, was strangely comforting.

"Solution. This unit will go to the control deck and examine." A display popped up in front of Inez, and she saw herself for the first time. She was ashen, which made the dark bruises around her eyes stand out even more. She realized for the first time that she wasn't in her jumpsuit, just an undershirt and shorts.

After a moment, she realized what it meant. "Yes, you go to the command deck, and show me what's there."

It took about fifteen minutes for Doc to make its way to the control deck. She'd been treated to views of empty corridors and rooms. There was a kitchen that she could probably make use of once she had some idea of what was going on. There was also an exercise facility that looked like it hadn't been used in years. Finally, there was a door that read, "Command." It opened, and the medic-bot trundled in.

"Doc, can you pull up when the other three ships arrived?"

Data filled the display. It looked like the Company ships arrived first, probably because of her message to them. One ship was administrative. The other was a heavier cargo ship. They were probably planning to transfer the cargo off the damaged hold unit onto this ship. If any of the cargo survived the crash.

No, if she survived, those cargo crates would be practically pristine. The Company did not fuck around when it came to cargo. She assumed that it would be the same with living cargo. But, hold on.

"Doc, which of the Company ships is still here?"

It showed her a visual of the ship. It was the cargo carrier. When the Company came, it would be to protect the cargo. So why leave the cargo and the cargo carrier, but depart in the admin ship? And why was there a Free Earth ship here when she arrived? "Are there a/v records of the Free Earth ship arriving?"

The data feed was replaced by a recording showing the Free Earth ship, a smallish frigate, docking. Based on the timestamp, the Free Earth arrived just over an hour after the Company did. The view changed to inside the station, where she saw a half-dozen marines file out, led by a Colonel. Their drab green uniforms with black insignia were designed to allow them to blend in nearly anywhere, draw no attention to themselves. That was not the effect that uniform had on Inez.

The video changed, and she saw Hymie Fang welcome the marines onto the control deck. The Colonel, without saying a word, had him in a headlock, choking him into unconsciousness.

"What the fuck?" She was used to ruthless. Sixteen years with the Admiral taught her that. This was somehow worse than if they'd just shot him. This, along with his not being on the waystation anymore, meant they had plans.

The video jumped forward to her own rig's arrival. The data feed said that once the eight people (marines and Fang) had departed, no one else entered the station before she crashed into it.

She watched the bottom of her rig scrape the top of the docking ring. Inez couldn't help but cringe at that. She then saw about twenty balls of light attach to the sides of the rig, pulling it off the station, and maneuvering it into position at the dock. The mechanotrons started scanning, and found her in the cabin. The airlock was opened, and one of the machines entered, and half a minute later emerged with her cradled in its manipulator arms.

She allowed herself a moment of bitterness, that machines had shown her kindness when no one moved from any of the other ships. She watched the mechanotron lay her body onto the bed in the medbay, and at the apparent direction of the Doc, gingerly remove the exosuit from her body. It then carefully backed away and the Doc went to work.

She was getting sucked into watching it work, and had to shake her head to clear it, which actually led to another wave of nausea. Concussion, right. "Doc, do we have any information about what led to the other ships departing?"

She could hear audio chatter between the Company and the Free Earth. It was hard to make out, since it was partially encrypted, but the tones were not friendly.

The Free Earth ship launched a torpedo. The Company ship wouldn't have had time to undock if it was a normal torpedo, but it was slow moving, almost furtive. The untrained eye might think it was a probe, but neither Inez nor the Company had untrained eyes.

The brown ship detached from the ring and started to travel away, its singularity drive spinning, showing it was about to jump immediately to light speed. A half second before it left, the torpedo sent out a pulse of some kind. The data feed reported that all twenty crew on the admin ship, and the five crew on the cargo ship, were dead instantly. The drive kicked in, and the admin ship took off on a journey of the dead.

"Fucking fuck. Doc, I should be dead."

"Negative. The medbay is shielded against the type of radiation released in that attack. Also shielded against scanners."

Inez felt like she was going to cry. These automatons had shown her more kindness in the last twelve hours than any stranger had in her entire life.

She saw the marines leaving the ship again. This time, they were wearing respirators and heavy weapons, which made them less human than they had seemed before. But why respirators? They hadn't removed the air from the station.

Then she noticed an indicator on the bottom of the display. The radiation was not as lethal as it had been right after the torpedo attack, but it was still pretty dangerous. This must be why the medic-bot had kept her from leaving the medbay. "First do no harm."

The marines went straight for her ship. They must be after the slaves for some reason. She was pretty sure that being inert, they wouldn't be affected by the radiation, but again, there was another pang of guilt. She was going to have to deal with delivering them right into Free Earth hands. She still wasn't sure what she was going to do about the whole thing, but their fate was out of her hands now.

Or... not? The marines broke into teams of two, and through the eyes of the mechanotrons she could see them ransacking her ship. Shit, they weren't there for the slaves at all. They wanted that data cube. Why the fuck did they kill the Company employees? She would have just given them the damn thing.

However, they emerged from the rig empty handed. She was glad she'd thought to stow it under one of the floor plates. They were an obvious spot to stick contraband (which she was sure a previous owner did), but these marines didn't know smuggling from legitimate trade.

Angry and annoyed, the marines went around the rest of the station, looting and pillaging as they went. She pushed the speed of the replay up to watch them go around the station. It took them about an hour, and then they went back to their ship. The ship left the station at that point.

Motherfuckers. Somehow, she didn't know how, they missed the medbay. She would almost certainly be dead otherwise.

"Doc, how long until I can leave?"

"Station systems are purging radiation. Mechanotrons also purging radiation from your ship and the Company ship. Overall, expect 28 minutes to nominal safety."

"And how long until my ship is ready?"

"Three days, five hours, 52 minutes."

It was going to be hard enough to track the Free Earth ship, and harder still if she waited that long. There was the other ship, though. It was a heavy cargo carrier, but at the moment it had no cargo or attached cargo bays. It was capable of a lot of things her rig was not able to pull off, even if her rig was in great condition.

Inez looked around the room. To one side was a wall of diagnostic tools. On the other, a smooth white wall, but Inez could tell it was actually cabinets. Something about the false walls like this had always been obvious to her.

She got up and went over to that wall and pressed next to a faint vertical line. There was a click, and then a door swung out. Pain killers, anti-radiation drugs, bandages, everything she could need and a lot more she had no idea what it was.

She grabbed the rad-suppressor and jabbed the needle into her neck before she could give it much thought. It stung like a bastard. She could feel it spreading, a wave of cold and hot over her body. More nausea followed the waves and she took several deep breaths to get it under control.

She found an unopened package of fifty pain tabs, and went to stuff them into her pocket. That's when she remembered that she was just in underclothes. She held onto the pain killers and grabbed another rad-suppressor in case she needed it. The door swung open as she approached, and she stepped out into the dark corridor.

She followed the signs to the docking ring, and located her rig. The docking arm was attached to the left side of the drive core. Inez checked the air pressure and was glad to see there was some. She opened the door to the arm and followed the fifty meters to her ship's airlock. Again, there was air pressure, so she stepped onto the ship.

Ten minutes later, she crawled back out, wearing a fresh jumpsuit and a carrying a bag slung over her shoulder. "Alright, the other ship is…" she did a little turn, figuring out the direction based on the details from the video feed. "To the right. Got it."

Inez found the docking arm controls and used her Company credentials to gain access. "Glad that worked," she said under her breath. It wasn't like she had a plan B.

The Company ship was a lot like her rig, only bigger. The non-cargo portion was a squat triangle, with the singularity drive at the back tip, and the control cabin at the front and to the right. It was large enough to have a crew, so in addition to the captain's seat, there was a helmsman, an engineer, a full-time medic, and a cargo specialist.

And here they all were, in their seats, covered in sores and already starting to desiccate. They all died nearly instantaneously, which was the only mercy in their deaths.

There was a mechanotron doing some patching up in the corridor outside of the cabin. Inez ordered it inside and had it take the bodies to the bunks, starting with the helmsman. Once the seat was empty, she sat down and checked the ship's sensors. It looked like the Free Earth ship was heading towards the nearest loyal system, about 300 light years away. She undocked from the waystation and piloted about twenty kilometers out. She then decoupled from the cargo hold. It was just going to slow her down.

She set a course for the star system, spun up the thrusters, and punched the FTL.

• ▪ ▪ ▪ ▬▬▬▬ ▪ ▪ ▬ ιι((◉))ιι ▬ ▪ ▪ ▬▬▬▬ ▪ ▪ ▪ •

Inez had sort of forgotten how gentle faster than light travel could be. Even when it was working properly, her rig wasn't the smoothest ride. This was a Company ship, though, and they were kept in top working order. The singularity in this ship's drive core would be a fair amount more dense, giving it better control and higher speeds. It was beautiful and scared the shit out of her.

Inez was about a third of the way to the system where she assumed the Free Earth were taking Hymie. She hadn't even really given it a thought. As soon as she saw them take him, she knew she was going to have to rescue him.

How was that so obvious that it wasn't a choice for her? She didn't know him. But somehow, he got caught in something between Free Earth and the Company, and that was her fault.

She was taking advantage of the gravity and running hot water and soap, taking a shower for the first time since well before this began. Her rig didn't have a shower, so she was mostly able to do this on the short stops between drop-offs and pick-ups. While traveling, the best she could do is a wipe down. It was 2734, dammit, they should have figured out a way to make this available universally by now.

Inez was able to look at herself better in the shower than in the medbay. Her torso was covered in bruises, and the water coursing over her body was helping to loosen knots in her back and neck. She had found a personal stash of beer belonging to one of the crewmembers, and was on her third just while showering.

She was even washing her hair, as problematic as that could be. It was thick and kinky and unruly, but it had also absorbed every rotten smell from the past three days, so that won out. Someone on this ship liked really flowery soaps, so the tang was being replaced with lavender. There were worse things to smell like.

Inez touched the control and the water turned off. She was blasted with air from all directions, pushing the water droplets away from her. Her hair became a globe of frizz, as the water evaporated from it. She wasn't looking forward to brushing it later.

She pulled clean underclothes from the bag she'd packed and got dressed. According to the clock, it would be a few more hours until she got within pinging range of the other ship.

● ▪ ▪ ▪ ▬▬▬▬ ▪ ▪ ▬ ıı((◉))ııı ▬ ▪ ▪ ▬▬▬▬ ▪ ▪ ▪ ●

This ship had a game room with an exercise machine, comfortable chairs, and a large video display for 2- and 3-dimensional entertainment. This would be great if it wasn't for the five dead people in the crew cabin.

Inez sat down on the cushioned bench in the game room, and pulled the data cube from her bag. She had a feeling the computer on this ship was a bit more powerful than her own. She plugged the lead into the cube, and it lit up. A display window popped up in front of her. She had the ship's computer run a diagnostic on the core.

It was still encoded, and the computer estimated that it would take 300 years and change to decode, but she could see more information about the data. For one thing this cube wasn't even one percent full. She didn't expect it to have a lot of data on it, but that was lower even than she was expecting. It's possible the ship was just setting out for a long term assignment, and if so, their orders would definitely be on this.

She didn't figure she'd be able to jump-start that 300 years, but maybe the brute force method would allow her to get something out of it. This was what they wanted. They'd probably interrogated Hymie, and not gently. He didn't know anything about the data core. It was her fault that he was even in this. She should have just left the beacon and let the Free Earth deal with it themselves.

But she wanted to make sure that there was no other danger to her out there. That was true, right? Or was that just what she wanted to believe? She'd be lying if she didn't admit that curiosity was part of it, but she wouldn't have taken it if she was just curious. And it's not like she had any idea the core would be anything other than a ship's log.

As soon as she saw it, she should have tossed it straight out the airlock. Instead, she plugged it into her computer. Was that how they knew she had it? Well, then they'd definitely know she had it now.

She looked in some cubbies and found similar, but much smaller, cubes that held game programs. She found one with a familiar word printed on it: "Тетрис". The block game. Well, if that wasn't a sign. She grabbed a dozen different games and stuck them in her bag. Then she plugged in Тетрис.

If they knew, then they'd be coming for her. If they didn't, then it was going to be a good ten hours still. She had time to play a game.

7

Inez was back in the command cabin. Ten minutes ago, the Free Earth ship's ping reached her. They weren't being stealthy, they wanted her to find them. She knew it was them because the call sign in the ping was the same as the one at the station.

They had stopped a few light years short of the system they'd been headed toward. Their sensors were far better than anything she had, so they probably saw the ship coming, and knowing they'd killed everyone on the ship, made the only logical leap.

Or, they knew she was alive, had let her live, and were using Hymie as bait to get the data core back. They wouldn't use traditional energy weapons, since they didn't want to damage it. They would almost certainly use the same sort of radiation torpedo. The ship's computer had been very helpful in analyzing the radiation, and determining the safest place in the ship for her. The mechanotron that was along for the voyage was busy adding rad shielding. She was not going to go out that way.

The ship's computer was a variant on the combat computers used in older Free Earth ships, so she programmed in a few evasive maneuvers, the main one was to put the majority of the ship between her and the radiation torpedo, but there were a few others.

One of the battles her mother had taught her about, when she was six, was between the Hands and the Free Earth. The Hands came in under a flag of truce (entirely computer to computer, so there was still no detail about the Hands to learn anything about them). The Free Earth, sensing their chance, and under the direct orders of Brother Xavier, dropped out of light speed and immediately fired torpedoes and energy weapons where their sensors showed the ship being.

Except it wasn't there. The lead ship just managed to get that message off to GalCom, when ten Hands ships appeared, and the entire fifteen ship Free Earth fleet was reduced to scrap. Her mother's lesson in that was don't trust a flag of truce, and don't be an asshole if someone tries to call for a truce. The Hands were testing the Free Earth, and the Free Earth failed.

Inez sent a ping back to the other ship. This was probably not going to work. Almost certainly not going to work. There wasn't any way this was ever going to work.

On the other hand, it would all be over soon. If she ran away, Hymie would end up dead, she would be forever on the run, and she still had at least 18,000 slaves to worry about. Making a stand, no weapons, no escape, nothing but a plan, well, maybe she would finally get hers.

"You can't fix anything if you're dead," she heard Ihuoma say. "I can't fix anything now anyway," she said, to no one.

The console beeped, and Inez shook her head to drive off the spell. They wanted to talk. It was show time.

She pressed the flashing button and a display popped up in front of her. It was the Colonel, flanked by two marines, and in the back, she could see Hymie being held up by more marines.

"Inez Stanton."

"Colonel..." she replied, keeping her voice as neutral as she could.

"Abram Hynes. Hmm, yes. Your file indicates you would be familiar with the military. Your file actually makes for very interesting reading."

"I'm sure yours does, too. Do you usually go around murdering employees of the Tenth Great and Glorious Browns Company?"

"They were," he paused here, as though he was looking for an appropriate colloquialism, "collateral damage."

"And you wonder why people hate you."

"Oh, no. We are well aware of our place in the galaxy. And of yours."

It was a real struggle to keep from rolling her eyes. She pulled the data cube out of her bag so they could see it.

"I assume this is what you're after?" She casually tossed it from hand to hand. She bobbled it a couple times, which was not intentional, but the panicked look from the Colonel told her plenty.

"We will take it from you by force, if necessary."

"I have no doubt that you will. I'm stopping here. I'm not going to drop into an ambush in a ship with no weapons and no shields. You feel free to come meet me." She closed the display to end the conversation.

She'd managed to get through it without blacking out, which she figured was a victory in itself. She slumped back in the chair, and brought the ship to a stop. She was nowhere near anything.

Another ping from the Free Earth confirmed that they were en route to her location. She had less than an hour to get ready, but given her plan, she didn't want to get in there any more than five minutes prior.

She did have things she could do, though. She went to the locker room next to the airlock, and pulled out an exosuit. Unlike her, the Company kept their suits powered up, so she spent the next twenty minutes pulling the suit on, making sure all the seals were in place and correct, and that she had plenty of oxygen available if she needed to activate the helmet. These were rated for higher radiation space, so it should provide a little more protection against their weapon than just being in the singularity room.

She hated this plan. But the singularity room's shielding would be superior to any other place on the ship. It might not even need the additional plates that the mechanotron was installing outside the door.

She had poked her head into the room soon after heading out, and it was just as unnerving as the one on her own ship. Given the amount of dust that was on the catwalk, the engineer for this ship also avoided coming in as much as possible. When she was still alive.

It was a larger singularity, and thus the sphere was larger. The catwalk didn't just go around the outside of the room, but actually crossed the singularity itself. This was allegedly so that readings could be taken from within it, but since it existed beyond three dimensional space, it required highly sensitive equipment that couldn't be kept long-term on a ship or it would lose calibration.

Still, according to the computer, it would be completely safe for her to stand there. Safe physically. Gods knew what it would do to her mind.

The computer beeped at her. Five minutes left. This was going to happen.

● ■ ■ ■ ▬▬▬▬▬ ■ ■ ▬ ιι((◉))ιι ▬ ■ ■ ▬▬▬▬ ■ ■ ■ ●

In space, everything is very small. When you're right next to something on a planet, it can take up your entire field of vision. In space, even at the same size or bigger, it's dwarfed by space itself.

A speck appeared near another speck, and an infinitesimal speck departed the one that just appeared and crossed to the one that had been there. Space was completely indifferent to this activity.

On the stationary speck, Inez slammed the door to the singularity room shut. Even through this shielding, they'd be able to see that she was alive, so she walked out to the center of the room, across the catwalk, directly into the center of

fifteen years old and
child skipping in the grass
holding her hand for
hundredth time the fist hit

crying for her momma
don't let him see
Ihuoma in the casket
drawing pictures of ships
bad idea, baby, bad idea
making love in the cave
Sara putting on her
fucking fuck
when the lights went out
blast
blast
blast

into the center of the writhing mass of the singularity. Fuck, that was disorienting.

She had a view of the torpedo, with the cloud of radiation illustrated in red. She knew they were going to have more they could use on her, but she had the data core in with her, so she had a good idea of what their plan would be.

The frigate pulled up beside the cargo carrier, and a docking ring extended out to meet it. The airlock was only about ten meters from the drive core, but there were about a hundred meters of corridors to go through to get there. Unlike her own rig, where this plan would never work.

What the fuck is she talking about? There's no plan. So they board the ship, find that she's not anywhere else, then what? Fighting marines? She hated them, she didn't want to kill them. Or have them kill her, which was far more

Admiral reaches for his
little cat in the street, licking
18,000, that's far too many
"What do you mean, princess?"

infrasonic

237 years old? That must

far more likely. Goddammit, that was awful. She usually tried to avoid looking directly at the singularity, but that wasn't an option here. Still, she tried focusing on the display of marines coming over. Fifteen, from what she could see. A frigate crew was about 30, they wouldn't have room for many additional, so the navy crew was probably about 15, assuming not all the marines had come over, and probably led by a Commander or even Lieutenant Commander, if a Marine Colonel was in command.

The marines floated across the docking ring and keyed in the override code to get into the airlock. They somehow all fit going in at once, and the bulkhead door closed the docking tube off behind them. The time, as tenuous a concept as that was in the middle of the singularity, was now.

8

The data cube hung heavy in her bag. She could see the mechanotron about six meters away, looking dormant. She knew better, though. She just didn't know if this was going to work.

A marine rounded the corner. They weren't wearing respirators, so they were probably hopped up on anti-rad drugs, which had the added effect of pumping up adrenaline. Inez was still in the exosuit, and that seemed to be keeping a lot of the remaining radiation out. The marine stopped short, seeing the mechanotron. He waved his arms in front of the automaton, and not seeing a reaction exhaled and turned to continue down the corridor.

Inez tapped a control on her suit, and the mechanotron whipped its manipulator arm across the back of the marine's head, and he crumpled to the ground soundlessly. Inez tapped another control, and she could see a medical readout. He was alive, but with a pretty good concussion. Nothing a night in the medbay couldn't fix, but for now, he was out.

The mechanotron lifted the unconscious marine gently and carried him into the singularity room. If he woke, the disorientation in that room should keep him from going anywhere.

In the time she waited for it to come back, Inez watched some of the movements of the marines. There weren't a lot of solo adventurers here, mostly groups of two or three.

She tapped another control, and the mechanotron moved ahead of her, steadily down to the next corner. Two marines were already at that corner, and the machine caught both of them at the neck, one in each grasper. It pushed them up against the bulkhead, choking them until they passed out.

Inez stayed put again until the robot returned from depositing the two with their comrade, and checked where the rest were. There were three in the game room, two in the command cabin, and two in the bunks. She ordered those three cabins sealed, and removed the air until the marines in there were knocked out. She watched the lights showing their locations on her map slowly go from bright red to dark red. Still alive, but unconscious.

That only left five. Even more importantly, nobody was dead. Was that important? It seemed important. It seemed like the least she could do, given everything. She would be the bigger person. She heard the first comms chatter since the marines came aboard, then. "What's going on over there? This shouldn't be taking so long."

Well, that was new. The Colonel was rattled. Those unfamiliar with military command wouldn't necessarily hear it, but Inez had heard it before. She heard it right before she pulled the trigger on the Admiral's infrasonic blaster and took his head clean off. Accustomed to precision, to everything following its standard procedure, when things go south and you haven't prepared for it, that's when that waver would come.

The Colonel had that controlled panic sound now. She knew he could see that ten of his marines had been rendered unconscious, that this simple plan of his was falling apart. That some little girl was ruining everything.

But he hadn't planned. He didn't even have them taking the simplest of precautions, of using respirators, which would have rendered half of her plan moot. She knew she'd gotten lucky there, but there was no point in depending on luck for the rest of this.

Five marines. The first one was just around the corner. She heard the woman speaking, both over the comms, and because she was nearby. "Sir, she must still be alive."

"No shit, Corporal. Fix that."

Inez tapped the control, and the mechanotron zipped silently around the corner, and she heard the thud of the Corporal hitting the wall. Ten seconds later, there were two more thuds. She checked her display, and two more were down. She moved as quietly but quickly as possible down the hall and rounded the corner. She saw three unconscious bodies, but what pulled her gaze was the mechanotron. One of the marines had managed to get a shot off, and there was a hole in the side of its carapace, fist sized, right where its battery was.

"Fuck," she said under her breath. This was going to make the rest of her plan much harder.

She checked where the other two were. One was trying to get into the command cabin, and the other was coming straight towards her. She ducked into a closet. She was going to have to time this exactly right. She was sure that the marine coming her way would have their blaster out. Three meters away. Two. One.

Inez launched herself out of the closet, catching the marine off guard. The infrasonic blaster tumbled out of her hand and clattered away. The marine got a few jabs in on Inez's ribs, which felt like they must be broken again. This was going badly.

Inez used to wrestle with some of the slave boys, and she could feel her muscles remembering some of the moves. She managed to get an arm around the other woman's neck, and used the pivot point to quickly get her feet on the wall at hip level, and pushed off. Momentum carried them to the opposite bulkhead, where the woman slammed her head. Her eyes crossed a little, and she crumpled to the ground.

Inez looked over the woman (no, girl, gods, how young were they recruiting now?) and double checked the scan to make sure she was still alive. There was only one left, and no way to sneak up on them at all. The command cabin was at the end of a long corridor that went along the front of the vessel, with some single-entry cabins on one side, and the connection for the cargo hold on the other. She could only hope that the last marine was too busy trying to get into the command cabin that she wouldn't be noticed until it was too late.

She stepped down the corridor as quietly as possible. The man was intent on the door controls. He'd pulled the wall plate off and appeared to be jamming wires recklessly in different slots trying to force open the door. She noticed that he was doing it bare-handed. He wasn't trained, she could tell, so he really seemed to be a bit panicked, hoping to hit on something out of luck, something that would keep the Colonel from shoving him out the nearest airlock.

She realized that fate for him didn't bother her that much. She wasn't going to try to kill him, but working for the sort of person the Colonel seemed to be was almost certainly going to reduce his life expectancy.

She stopped short, about four meters away. This plan might not work after all. If the Colonel was that much of a bastard, then the whole hostage exchange thing might be moot.

She heard a buzz from the wall panel, and the marine swore. That's why you wear gloves when you're doing electrical work, dumbass. Oh, right, she thought, and tapped out a command on her suit. A bright flash filled the hall, and the marine was suddenly on top of her, and they were both rolling on the floor.

No, she was rolling. He was out. She checked his pulse, which was there. Good. Fifteen down, all still alive.

Inez unlocked the door to the command cabin and stepped over the three passed out marines. She pulled up a public information channel and searched for Colonel Hynes. A few news stories over the years detailing his later career, but there was a twenty-year period where he seemed to cease to exist. He was black ops, she would stake her rig on it.

This would explain the cavalier attitude toward torturing Hymie, especially knowing that he wouldn't actually know anything. That was almost certainly done after they found her following them.

Right. Research time was done. She opened a comms channel to the frigate.

"Colonel Hynes. You know, that wasn't very sporting."

"Miss Stanton. You surprise me again." She noticed some colonial accenting in his voice, this time. It was probably a hold over from his black ops days, taking out nascent rebellions (she assumed, since there was nothing on him).

"Your marines are all alive, Hynes. I know what you're after, and you can take the fucking thing. All you had to do was ask." Inez wasn't positive she was telling the truth there, but at this moment it was as true as she could be.

"I wouldn't expect mercy from someone with your... background," he said, with a sneer.

"A slave?"

"A murderer. Cotton was a mentor to me."

"Oh, fuck you. Seriously, fuck you straight to hell." Inez took a deep breath. "Show me Hymie Fang."

"Miss Stanton, you are in no position to make a demand."

"I have the data core. I have no idea what's on it," she said, and she pulled it out of her bag. She tossed it from hand to hand, watching the Colonel's eyes following it. "No idea. These things are kinda fragile, though. I mean, it'll take a bit of a beating, but if I drop it on a corner," she made a shattering noise.

"So you propose trading my marines and the data core for one man?"

Inez sighed. She bit her lower lip and looked up, and then shrugged. "Yeah, that's about it."

"And if I say no?"

Inez made the shattering noise again. "I mean, it's your call. Things break all the time out here in space. You probably saw my rig. You should have seen how little was left of the ship where I found this." Toss. "Rendered to bits by something. I'm fairly certain that it was something from that ship that hit me to begin with." Toss. "You probably want to know what did that."

She could tell he was doing the math. She knew that he would be coming to the conclusion she wanted him to.

"So here's how it is. You bring Hymie over here. You, yourself, unarmed, along with whoever you need to get your people. Wear an exosuit. You stay here long enough to get your people back. Your docking ring gets retracted. Then, and only then, do I give you this data cube." She wasn't quite sure she believed this was going to go how she was explaining it, but better to sound confident.

"Then, to make sure you don't just kill us afterward, you will float over to your ship, between you and us, in just that exosuit. Your ship picks you up, and we're gone."

"Fine," he spat out, and killed the channel.

Military efficiency meant that within ten minutes the Colonel and a handful of crew had exited the frigate and were floating across to the cargo ship. Inez scanned the Colonel, and he didn't have a weapon on him. Inez had gathered all of the infrasonic blasters that the marines had brought over and sealed them in a biohazard bag. It would take better than thirty minutes for the bag to be opened, given that it was meant for highly contagious materials.

She greeted them at the airlock. The crew members were at the front, led by their ship's medic. At the back, the Colonel was holding up a barely conscious Hymie.

"Alright, let's get him to the patch up," she said, taking the young man under the shoulder. The ship had a small medical room that was really just a chair in a closet, but it had medical scanners and some first-aid supplies.

By the time she got him situated into the chair, the first few marines had already been transferred to the frigate. She turned to face the Colonel. He was a good quarter meter taller than she was, and she did her best to not be intimidated.

"So, you knew my father?"

"I knew Cotton Ringwald. Your owner."

"Ex-owner," she corrected him. "Former. Since his death, I was legally freed."

He was looking at her like she was something he wanted to scrape off his boot. The more time he spent in her presence, the more disgusted he seemed.

"But yes, he was my father. Forced himself on my mother over and over again. He was such a charmer." Her fingers involuntarily curled into fists. The old anger was threatening to overtake her.

"Did you know my mother? Looked like me, but skinnier and prettier? He killed her with his bare hands."

A look passed over his face. She wasn't sure quite what that look meant. Recognition? Anger? Impending cardiac event? Whatever, she had ceased caring almost as soon as the question occurred to her.

Hymie stirred a bit at this point, and Inez turned back to the chair. "It's okay, bud. We'll get you patched up." She punched some buttons on the medsuite control and she saw a readout of his various injuries. The most worrying was the brain bleed, so she gently pushed his head back into the chair and strapped it in place so the medsuite could work on fixing it.

"You Free Earth types don't give a fuck about the lives of anyone who doesn't fly the flag, do you?"

This seemed to push him out of whatever space his head was in. "True patriots will do what is necessary to protect the Free Earth. If some heads get cracked along the way, that's the price of freedom."

"Oh, for fuck's sake. I. Was. A. Slave. I was awarded my freedom, but even then, I am not free. I am never free."

"Awarded your freedom. The bastard daughter of my friend's wife hardly has a claim as the heir."

"It's good for you that you're in your exosuit already. I don't want to kill anyone, but I am sorely tempted to push you out the airlock." Inez was a little surprised to find that it wasn't a lie. This asshole had managed to push her buttons.

She managed to take a calming breath. "You know, all this time, I'd figured that you were after the slaves in my cargo hold. Slaves that I have to deliver if I'm going to keep my freedom. I thought this whole thing was a test put forth by the Free Earth to make sure I could be kept in line. But you don't give a shit about them."

A call came over the comms system then. "Colonel, we've got everyone off but you."

"Thanks, Ensign," Hynes said, back to professional.

Inez verified this though the ship's computer and turned back to the Colonel. "So, you're up now."

"FES Gleason, retract the docking ring."

They could feel the ring detach from the hull, and Inez followed her foe through the corridors to the airlock. She opened the inner door, and prodded him through. Finally, she took the data core from her bag and handed it to him. "Here's your precious, worth twenty-seven lives, not to mention the several hundred on the dreadnought, fucking data cube. I imagine it won't impact your ability to sleep."

"I know you think I'm a monster. You're probably not wrong." A crease went across his dark brow. "Everything I've done, I would do it again. Even, well, I doubt we'd be here if it wasn't for one stupid night at Cotton's. Yes, I remember your mo--."

Inez slammed the inner door control to shut him off. She didn't look to see if he'd put his helmet up before opening the outer door. She watched him pulled out into space. He seemed to still be alive, so she sent the command to the computer to take them out of there.

9

She was back to being confined in the medbay. However, so was Hymie. Right now, they were waiting for the Company to come and collect their dead. She'd given them a full report of the incident, and their response was muted support for what she had done. The company wasn't evil, but they weren't exactly actively good either.

"How's your head?" she asked the proprietor. She knew that most of the damage had already been healed. It had been about ten hours in the chair on the ship, and then another twelve here on the waystation under the care of the medic-bot.

"I am aware of it. I don't like that." The false obsequiousness that he'd shown when they first talked was gone. This was the actual Hymie.

"How does a Sinodiasporadic get a name like Hymie, anyway?"

"How does someone as dark as you get the name Stanton?"

"Got it. Family."

"No one I've ever met is one thing only."

Inez sighed. "Sorry, I suck at small talk."

Hymie chuckled, and immediately regretted it.

"Look, I'm getting sprung in a few hours, and my rig is about ready to go. I still have to take care of my delivery."

"You have to get those slaves where they're going."

Inez hadn't told him, but then, he was neither stupid, nor was he fully unconscious when she was talking to Hynes.

"Yeah, I do. I hate it. But I do."

He didn't say anything. He was definitely conflicted about the while thing. He had to know that slaves came through his station regularly, and she guessed that did not sit well with him.

"This is a fight, Hymie, but it's not my fight. It can't be. Not right now."

The quiet of the medbay hung over them now like a dark cloud. Hymie sighed now. "Thanks for coming after me. You could have just waited until your ship was fixed and took off, but you didn't."

"Well, thank you for having the automatons in place to take care of me when I came crashing in. These aren't standard bots, are they?"

"I spend a lot of time on my own. We're not on a major shipping lane now, which we were when my mom bought the place, so I have a lot of time to tinker."

"So, I have to ask, why isn't the auto-dock working?"

"Well, I needed parts from somewhere. When the transmission arm got ripped off, it was easier to scavenge it for parts than to make it work again. Not my greatest idea, looking back."

"The Company will get here soon. You should talk to them about repairing it. I imagine they'll be grateful for your part in this." Actually, she didn't know if they would or not, but considering their losses on this, it was probably true.

"Anyway, you should probably rest. Too much thinking will slow the brain healing." Inez laid back on her bed and closed her eyes.

She woke up with a cold metal prod on her forehead. Immediately, she tried to shift into a fight posture, but she was being held in place. She opened her eyes, and the sensor package of the medic-bot was gazing down at her.

"You really need to learn some bedside manners," she mumbled, her heart rate slowing back down to a normal level. The restraining beams cut off, and she was able to move again. She looked over at Hymie, who was out cold. She checked the time.

"You're here to tell me it's time to get going?"

"Affirmative. Your ship is also ready to go. All necessary systems have been restored, and the upper bulkhead of the cargo hold has been patched."

"What's the bill?"

The sensor package tilted again.

"How much do I owe to the waystation?"

"Maintenance to your ship and to yourself has been provided free of charge."

Inez looked over at Hymie again. She got up, now, and walked over and kissed his forehead. "Sorry for all the trouble." The young man didn't stir.

"I'm starving, Doc. Does this place have any food?"

Inez sat down at a networked station with a bowl of hot potatoes and gravy, and brought up her account. There was another message from the Company, thanking her for ensuring that no further casualties had happened. She checked her balance, and they had given her the two thousand euan, but they had also charged her for the damage to their other ships, so in the end, she only got 350 euan. She sent 50 to the waystation as a tip.

The potatoes were salty and thin, but they tasted amazing right now. If there was anything better than mashed potatoes when the rest of the galaxy was tearing itself to pieces, she didn't know it. The gravy was meat-based, but not an earth meat. She couldn't really place it.

There was a message from an unmarked sender, and that never meant anything good. Better to open it here instead of out there, where a virus could really wreak havoc.

"Inez,

"You do remind me of your mother, you know. She was a spitfire, and I know that she was not well treated by Admiral Ringwald. She was beautiful, coffee dark, proud, and she was the first woman I loved.

"I won't chase after you. After all, I have what I came for, and more. This data on the core will help the Free Earth more than you could ever conceive, and we will be more powerful for it.

"And you will still be out there, making things messy. Our paths may yet cross again, and if they do, we'll deal with this in that murky future.

"You have your freedom. I have my duty.

"Farewell,

"Your Father."

Inez restrained herself from punching the station, barely. That bastard. Fucking slave fetishizing, murdering, aging ball sack of shit. And he wanted to pretend they had a connection? Someone she hadn't heard of until two days ago wanted to claim to be her father?

And why the fuck would he want that? She killed her last father. She wanted to kill him. The whole shit show, start to finish, on this one man? That was something she could focus her rage on.

No. No, that was stupid. That was angry-Inez who she had buried a decade ago. That wasn't who she was anymore. That wasn't who she was allowed to be now.

No, it didn't matter who was her father, genetically speaking. She'd never had a father, so this was literally no different from the last twenty-seven years of her life. With the Admiral gone, it's not like this Colonel was going to fill a vacuum.

It was time to get going. The cargo wouldn't deliver itself.

The rig was clean. No, that wasn't quite right. It was like new. The walls were a brighter shade of brushed metal, the floor (with working gravity) was practically slippery. She opened the door to the storage room, except that it wasn't being used for storage. Her bunk was in there now, with working cubbies to store things like her clothes and personal items. The only thing in the room from when it had been the storage room was the exosuit locker, and a quick look there told her they had patched the suit up and had it fully powered.

She set her bag down on the bunk, and pulled out the Тетрис cube. It didn't have the game on it now, after she'd replaced it with the encrypted data on the dreadnought's core. She wasn't going to plug it in, though, in case the thing that sent out the homing ping copied over as well.

Inez opened the door to the cab, and she was greeted with all new consoles, it looked like. Saint Camilia was gone, but so was the bullet hole. Everything gleamed.

If she was being honest, it was a little unnerving.

In the corner of the cab, there was a box. She touched the top of the box, and it split open. A polished stainless steel manipulator arm, followed by a second, unfolded. The second arm had a card on it.

"This is the mechanotron you took to rescue me. It's very loyal, and goes by 'Lui'. Take care of it, and it will take care of you.

"Thanks,

"Hymie."

Dammit, she was not going to cry. She took a deep breath. "Hi Lui." The manipulator arms waved.

Right. Getting out. "Computer, put us back on course for the delivery."

"Apstiprinoši, kapteini."

Inez looked back down at the mechanotron. "Seriously?"

A message flashed up in front of her. "Mechanotrons are not programmed to change language circuits. You'll probably need an expert for that."

Of course. "Fine. Let's get out of here." The singularity powered up, and the rig pinched out of the orbit of the waystation.

Acknowledgements

Space is a vacuum, but Inez didn't come to life in one. Every story takes a village to come to life, and I had a great village behind me.

Chronologically, my wife and her Tuesday night knitting group afforded me a lot of time for the writing. We'd both go out to the restaurant, she'd go off with her knitting friends, and I would go to a table by myself and bang out the words for an hour or so.

The Writer's Block Discord server (and all the great participants there) gave me a cargo hold's worth of support, encouragement, and snark. They were a huge help in getting me to "The End".

My beta readers, Jennifer, Nicole, Beth, Eleanor, Kate, Lynda, Stephanie, Kathy, Kim, Lisa, and, of course, Mary Ellen.

My editor, Kat Howard, gave me tons of great advice and pointed me to a few areas where I didn't do quite as well as I had hoped. Anything that's not great here is my fault, not hers.

Finally, thank *you*. Thank you for reading. You make it all worth it.

JS (Jeff) Carter Gilson
May, 2020

Translation

Just in case you want it, here are the translations for the rig's computer:

Page 1:
"Saluti, comandante." Italian. "Greetings, commander"
"Мы пострадали от мусора." Russian. "We were hit by debris."
"Rahtikotelossa." Finnish. "Cargo hold."

Page 2
"Les barrières tiennent." French. "The barriers are holding."
"Tilu dinten, di speed urang ayeuna." Sundanese. "Three days, at our current speed."

Page 3
"Pêgirtî, serwer." Kurdish. "Yes, Captain."

Page 6

"Tha luchd-dìon a 'putadh barrachd sprùilleach gu aon taobh." Scots Gaelic. "Deflectors are pushing more debris to one side"

Page 23
"Қоқысты болдырмас үшін курсты кенеттен түзету." Kazakh. "Sudden course adjustment to avoid debris."

Page 117
"Apstiprinoši, kapteini." Latvian. "Affirmative, Captain."

https://www.jscartergilson.com/

www.ingramcontent.com/pod-product-compliance
Lightning Source LLC
Chambersburg PA
CBHW022035170626
46808CB00003B/1219